MW01532779

I'M NOT AFRAID OF WOLVES

ALSO BY ERIN HAYES

THE COTTON CANDY QUINTET
How to be a Mermaid
I'd Rather be a Witch
I Do Believe in Faeries
I'm Not Afraid of Wolves
How to Talk to Ghosts (Halloween 2016)

THE HARKER TRILOGY
Damned if I Do
Damned if I Don't
Damned Either Way (Coming Fall 2016)

THE ELYSIUM LEGACIES
Death is but a Dream
Life is but a Nightmare (Coming Fall 2016)

Fractured
Jacob Smith is Incredibly Average
Open Hearts
The Royal Trade
The Solar Express
I Found My Rhino
Head Case: A Weird Science Romance (Coming Soon)

For my fierce writing and reading friends.
Don't be afraid to howl and let it all out.

CHAPTER 1

"C'MON, CHRISTINE, YOU NEVER DO ANYTHING fun."

I massaged my temples as I listened to my baby sister chide me for always working and never going out for a so-called "girl's retreat". I loved her to death, but she was relentless.

"Sara," I said, "you know I just got off a country-wide tour. I can't."

"It's the perfect time for you to come out with us."

Sara sounded smug, like she had expected my excuse. After all, I gave her an excuse every time she called. Nothing was ever relaxing with Sara though.

And this time, my excuse was the absolute truth. All I wanted to do was go to my house in Jacksonville, flop down on my bed, and sleep for a thousand years. Besides, with three new professional mermaids in the troupe, there was little chance of my boss, Neptune, giving me the time off. After ten years of working together, Neptune and I were more friends than coworkers, but there was such a thing as bad timing.

I had to get Sara to realize that.

Except, she got there ahead of me.

"Christine, please?" she asked. "Remember how fun your divorce party was?"

I snorted, my resolve softening. "That was a fun night," I conceded. Marrying Shane at age twenty had been the biggest mistake of my life and when I was finally free of that emotionally abusive relationship two years later…well, I went a little crazy. I'd just been hired by Neptune's World, and I wanted to celebrate this new lease on life. I dimly remembered a trip to Las Vegas and wearing my brand-new mermaid tail out in public.

Actually, I had to buy a new costume after that incident. That's the way anything with Sara goes: it turns out both amazing and a complete disaster.

"And that was almost ten years ago," Sara pressed.

"It was?" *Gah*, was it really?

"And you've just been working so hard since then. You really could use a break."

Damn, she was making sense. I combed a hand through my hair and let out a long sigh. I was thirty-one-years-old, and if I didn't have fun now, I'd wake up one day and realize that I was sixty years old without a good story to tell myself.

A part of me nagged that if that happened, it wouldn't be a bad thing. My relationship with Shane was a rocky one, and I had finally managed to convince myself that love wasn't for me.

A nice, quiet life. That's exactly what I wanted.

"Where is this retreat?" I asked, knowing I was going to regret this.

"Northeastern Georgia, near the Chattooga River." I had no idea where that was. "In the Chattahoochee National Forest. *Far* away from civilization. It's the perfect place to just forget it all."

That *sounded* like it would be the perfect vacation. Rural Georgia seemed like it would be a far cry from Jacksonville.

And maybe that was exactly what the doctor called for.

"Let me talk to my boss," I said through gritted teeth. I didn't know why they were gritted; did I think I was making a mistake, or was it from the horrible memories of my failed marriage?

"Yay!"

"I haven't committed to anything."

"Christine," my sister chided. "You have big, blue puppy dog eyes—"

"I do not."

"—and once you give him that look, he'll say, 'Sure, Christine, how much time do you want off?'" She paused for emphasis. "Please, make it happen. I need you." That last part came out in a whine. It was the same whine she used to persuade our parents to do anything when we were younger. Today, it struck a chord with me.

I exhaled, long and slow, screaming at myself to not agree to this. "I will try. No promises."

"Yaaay!" she cried again. "We're going to have so much fun. All of us girls."

I mentally groaned. "What do you mean 'all of us girls'?"

"You, me, Andrea, and Emily."

She said it like I knew who they were. And maybe, possibly, vaguely, I'd heard their names in the past. But this was the first time that Sara had mentioned anything about our girls' retreat being anything more than just the two of us.

I should have known.

Hope they are her good *friends*. I didn't like the idea of spending four days with complete strangers.

"Can't wait to see you, Christine!" she continued cheerily. "Call me back when you get the time off!"

"I—"

"Smooches!"

The line went dead. I looked at it, frowned, and then sighed.

What did I get myself into?

***

"You know, every time I give a mermaid time off, she decides to leave the troupe," Neptune said with a sideways grin. The old man was weather-beaten, sun-beaten—pretty much all sorts of "beaten" from hardships. He was missing teeth and a few marbles. But after everything, he had been something like a father and a best friend to me.

Actually, he was more like that crazy uncle that you were excited to see at Thanksgiving.

"Well, that's because Alaina had her baby," I said a little too defensively. "And Jordyn decided to stay home for her mom, and Tara—"

"Relax Christine, I'm just giving you a hard time."

My cheeks deepened. "I knew that."

I didn't.

I felt like I was letting him down. Neptune's Mermaids were taking off internationally. After an incident at the Houston Aquarium back in November, we were put on the map. Newspapers heralded us as conservationists who garnered appreciation for the sea through performance.

Frankly, I just liked the feeling of the water around me

He sighed and sat back in his chair and rubbed his face. "Do you think the new mermaids are okay to perform without your lead?"

I considered his question. I'd been with the mermaids for ten years now, and five of that was spent with Alaina and three with Jordyn. We'd gotten to know everyone's movements, how we worked, and were able to play off each other in the water. The new mermaids, Gabby, Murphy, and Liz, were all in their late teens and early twenties. Shelley had been with us four months now, and was very good at her job, and the other two weren't far behind.

They were good. But could they perform without me?

"No," I said. "I don't think they can."

Neptune smiled. "All right," he said at length. "Time off granted."

I blinked. "What? But I just said—"

"I know what you said Christine, and that's exactly why you should go on vacation." He chuckled. "I've seen them perform, I know they can do it without you. I was just wanting to see what you'd say."

"And if I had said they were all right?" I said, incredulous. "Would you have made me stay?"

"No, I still would have given you the time off."

I guffawed. "So why ask the question then?"

"Because you have to realize that you need a break. You've been working too hard." He got up from his spot at his desk—the old man never could sit for very long—and walked over to a side table that had a jade statue of a mermaid on it. I wasn't sure where his obsession with mermaids came from, but it was enough for him to start the mermaid troupe twenty years ago. He picked up the statue and started turning it over and over in his gnarled, callused hands.

He used to be a sea captain. That was probably where all of this came from.

"You've been putting a lot of pressure on yourself because everyone's been leaving," he said. "But I'm telling you, take some time off. You're not enjoying your performances as much as you should."

So he noticed.

"It's not that I don't enjoy it," I said. "It's just that…"

"It's because you're tired. I think this will be good for you. Come back refreshed and ready."

I almost snorted out loud. With Sara and her friends? It sounded like a great escape, but something would pop up. I was sure of it.

"And promise me you'll come back to the mermaid troupe," Neptune added, giving me a smile.

"Of course." *If Sara doesn't kill me first.*

"You're young, Christine," Neptune said. "You need to take advantage of it."

"I am."

"And you deserve a bit of happiness. Lord knows we all need happiness."

Neptune knew all about my divorce. He knew that I had to scrounge and fight my way out of that relationship. He knew of the abuse. I didn't tell him everything, but he probably knew more than anyone else alive.

It was a bad time in my life, and I was glad to be past that.

I gave a bittersweet smile, more at the memory than anything else. "I agree."

Neptune chuckled, which turned into a full body hacking. He barely, just barely, was able to put the mermaid statue back before he hunched over the side table with his coughing fit, using a hand to brace himself.

"Are you okay?" I asked.

"Yeah," he gasped between coughs. "I'm fine."

But he wasn't fine. He half-waddled, half-crawled to

the nearest seat, the spasms rocking him. I hurried to his fridge, grabbed a soda and popped the top, and handed it to him. He drank it greedily, tears streaming from his eyes.

"Thanks," he said, when he could speak again.

"What's that from?" I asked.

He shrugged. "Just getting old. I'm good."

I crossed my arms. "You need to see a doctor about that," I said, even though I knew his stance on doctors. I didn't know what it was about crotchety old men and doctors, but Neptune never wanted to see one.

He shook his head, which was the reaction I expected.

"I won't go on vacation unless you go see a doctor," I said.

"You drive a hard bargain."

"I'm just smarter than you."

He cracked a sardonic grin. "'Kay, 'kay, I will go see a doctor."

"Good." I wasn't' sure I believed him, but Neptune was pretty good about his promises.

"Now go," he said, waving me away. "You have a few more performances before next week."

"Yessir."

"And don't call me 'sir'."

You would think that after ten years of working with him, I knew not to call him that.

Still, I couldn't help the grin as I slipped out the door and went off to the dressing room. We had a performance in an hour.

Despite everything that was going against it, this vacation was going to be fun.

I was actually looking forward to it.

CHAPTER 2

AS I STOOD IN THE PICK-UP ZONE AT THE
Atlanta Airport, a car laid on its horn. The sound made me
jump with a cry and nearly drop my phone.

I'd been obsessively checking my messages to make
sure that the 1pm performance at Neptune's World went
all right. It was the last time I'd be able to see how our
shows would go, as I wouldn't have reception out in the
wilderness. I couldn't really take my work with me, even if
I tried.

The thought made me anxious and my fingers twitch.

I *really* needed a vacation if this was how I felt right
now.

"Christine!" a familiar voice cried. "Hey, Christine!"

I looked around, and jumped again as the horn sounded
once more. A packed Jeep pulled up to the side of the
curb, and Sara was in the driver's seat, grinning at me with
a wide smile.

"Long time, no see, sis!" she yelled with a mischievous
glint in her eyes.

Sara was only few years younger than me, but she
looked and acted like a girl in her early twenties. She had

my same dirty blond hair, although hers was pulled up into a severe ponytail. She wore a pair of sunglasses and a tank top.

To my absolute surprise, she looked like a serious camper.

There were two other women in the backseat, both lounging and chatting with each other. So they must have been Andrea and Emily. Suddenly, I felt like an outsider when these three were apparently good friends and close.

"Whoa, is that yours?" I asked, nodding at the Jeep.

She peered over her sunglasses with a good-natured smile. "Why do you sound surprised by that?"

"You were always more of a Mustang kind of girl."

She shrugged and caressed the steering wheel. "People change. This is my baby now."

Yes, they do. But Sara would never change, not deep down.

Sara pointed to the women in the back seat. "This is Andrea Smith, my neighbor."

The red-haired woman in the back seat smiled. "Nice to meet you!"

I grinned. "Nice to meet you too."

"And Emily Branton," Sara said, "I work with her at the PR company."

"Hey," the woman on the far side of the back seat side greeted me. With her black hair cut into a page style, she looked like the last person who would want to go camping. But she had a steeled, determined expression on, so I shouldn't be judging.

After all, this was one step away from glamping. It wasn't like we were doing Naked and Afraid.

"Is that all you brought?" Sara asked.

I looked down at my rolling carry-on bag. It had five changes of clothes, my bikini, and a pair of hiking boots to supplement the tennis shoes that I was already wearing. I also had two paperbacks tucked into my purse, but that was all I planned on needing. "Yeah?"

Sara pursed her cherry-red lips. "Christine, always the no-frills kind of girl. Even when it comes to roughing it."

I laughed; I used to be frillier and she knew it. A bad marriage made me really examine what was important in life. Although, right now, I wanted to look at my phone again. Evidence that I had become a workaholic in the meantime.

Maybe I had just changed my priorities in trying to do a complete 180 from where I was.

"Good thing I said I'd bring the supplies," Sara continued, breaking into my thoughts. "Where we're staying—it's not going to be the Ritz Carlton, but I think you'll be okay with that."

"I think I'll be just fine."

She jerked her thumb towards the back. "Bag goes in the trunk." Then she patted the front passenger's seat. "And you get to sit up here with me."

"Goody."

Sara snickered as I tossed my bag into the back. True to

her word, there were a lot of bags, including a giant cooler and totes filled with food.

This was really happening. And for once, it seemed like Sara was prepared for the trip ahead.

I opened the front passenger door. "Are we ready?"

Sara smirked. "Yep."

She threw the car into drive and we were off, on a three-hour trek north.

As the cityscape gave way to woodlands and mountains, I got one last text message from Murphy, one of the new mermaids, before I lost reception: *Have fun! Don't worry about us!*

That alone made me worry. More for myself than anything.

CHAPTER 3

"MUST PEE, MUST PEE, MUST PEE!"

Andrea nearly leapt out of the back seat of the Jeep to run into the gas station. I hoped there was no one in the stall—she'd been holding it for a long time since there were no other places to stop on the drive north. It wasn't the nicest gas station either, so I hoped the door at least latched.

"Whew," Emily said, getting out of the back seat of the car, stretching her legs. For the first time, I realized how tall she was. "It's been a while since I've had a road trip."

I shut the car door behind me. "You can sit in the front the rest of the way."

"Nah, I'm good." She gave me a smile, which made her look like a pin-up model with her black bob and her red lipstick. "You can deal with Sara's driving the entire way."

"I'm not a bad driver," Sara said, coming towards us. "I just live in Atlanta. What do you expect?"

"You're still driving like you're fighting eight lanes of traffic," Emily retorted.

Sara crossed her arms. "It's defensive driving."

"It's offensive to me." Emily patted her bag. "I'm going

inside to see if there's anything to drink. Do you ladies want anything?"

"Maybe," Sara said.

I shrugged. "I'll be in in a little bit. If there's anything I want, I'll get it then." If I was 100% honest, I'd have told her that I had to pee too. And maybe a little carsick, so I was glad Emily turned down my offer of taking the front seat. I always seemed to do better up there than in the back.

"You sure?" Emily pressed one more time.

I waved her away. "I'm good."

She nodded and turned and walked into the gas station. I also noticed that she was wearing four-inch heels. On a camping trip.

"She just broke up with her boyfriend," Sara explained as she stuck the nozzle into the gas tank. "She wanted to get away from it all."

"Like I did," I mused.

"And Andrea. And me." Sara got a faraway look in her eyes. "I'm really glad you're here, Christine."

"I needed it," I said. "I didn't realize how much."

"Are you okay?" Sara asked abruptly. Her question made my smile die on my face. "I, uh, mean with everything? You're just really quiet. All the time."

Sara only knew the top level of everything. She didn't know that I had been emotionally and physically abused in ways that I had never known were possible. She didn't know that I feared for my very life every night. And she didn't know that my actions from years ago still haunted me.

But her earnest look made me swallow down the torrent of sob stories and tears. Instead, I gulped down some air, nodded, and pasted a fake smile on my face.

"Yeah. I'm fine."

Sara watched me before taking my answer at face value. "You deserve to be happy, Christine."

"You sound like my boss."

She raised an eyebrow. "Your boss said that?"

"He's a nice guy. And no," I said, at her conniving glance, "he's in his sixties—*seventies* even. There's nothing there."

"Pity," she said, frowning. "Well, I guess there's got to be someone out there for you."

I could have asked what was up with her love life, but I figured that I would get an earful once we got to the cabin. Sara was a gossip, and I gossiped more in her presence than I had in a long time, but her question about my divorce had caught me off guard.

I felt sick, and it wasn't just from my car sickness.

"I'm going to go get some Gatorade," I announced, walking towards the gas station. "I need something to settle my stomach."

"Can you get me a frappuccino?" Sara asked.

I gave her a bewildered look and then glanced back at the gas station. "A frappuccino? Here?"

Sara loved her city-life conveniences. So why on Earth would she have the idea to go camping?

"There's those bottled ones," Sara said. "That'll do."

I highly doubted that this little gas station would have them, but I nodded. "All right, if I can find one."

"Five bucks says you will."

I didn't even acknowledge her bet as I jogged towards the entrance of the station. Rusted bars were on the outside of the shop, giving it a sinister, darkened appearance. It made me chuckle. *Isn't this how a lot of horror movies start?*

I pushed open the door, and the chime went off. The inside of the little mini mart wasn't a whole lot better, as the aisles were close together and stocked with very few items, and a strange smell hit my senses. But the attendant acknowledged me with a friendly wave.

"Hi, welcome to the Gas 'n Pass. Can I help you?" she asked.

I was glad that she was helpful. A quick look at her name tag identified her as Connie Sue. "Just looking for Gatorade and the bathroom."

"Bathroom's occupied," she said, indicating the back of the store. "But Gatorade's in that refrigerator."

"Thanks," I told her, just as the door to the bathroom opened, revealing Andrea. I strode over to her with a smile. "Is it safe?"

"It's clean," Andrea said, handing me the baton with the key. "So, yep."

"Cool," I said. I know I swim with marine animals for a living that poop and pee in the water, but there's something about public restrooms that make me feel a little squeamish.

"I'll be right out."

"Take your time," Andrea said. "I'm going to see if there's any snacks."

"We've got plenty of snacks," the all-too helpful attendant called from behind me. She must have been eavesdropping.

I opened the door to the single-seat unisex restroom, and, to my relief, it was clean. Small, but it didn't smell bad and I could do my business in here. I took my phone out of my purse and scrolled through my messages, stopping at the last one from Murphy an hour ago. It was five o'clock. They would have just finished up their performance for the day.

I made to text back, but then I remembered that I had no way of contacting her. No way of indulging in my worry.

Is this what I have become?

My fingers twitched at a thought that came to mind and I clicked on my gallery. I scrolled through all of the pictures, many of them showing me in my mermaid costume. I stopped on one picture that showed the four mermaids from November: Tara, Jordyn, Alaina, and me. We were a good group. We knew what we were doing.

Gah, I wished I didn't worry.

I scrolled through more images and I stopped at the last photo I'd saved of Scott and me together from Facebook. I was twenty-two, and while our relationship was going downhill even at that point, I looked young and happy. Not a care in the world.

That was before...

I shook the thought from my head. I should have deleted the photo a long time ago and erased any thoughts of regret, but I kept this. Why? After all, I was moving forward in my life now, and while it had taken me a decade of holding my head up high, I was able to do it now.

I was Christine Driver. And I was where I wanted to be in life.

"I'm alive, scum bag," I told his smug face through gritted teeth.

In a fit of inspiration, I deleted the photo, wiping away the last of Shane's hold on my life. Most of it, at least. That would have to do for now.

I waited a few heartbeats and then smiled. I felt lighter already.

A knock at the door made me jump and I nearly dropped my phone on the tile floor.

"Sorry!" I called. "I know I'm holding everyone up."

There was a pause, and then a voice said, "Take your time."

I blinked. That wasn't Sara nor Andrea nor Emily who spoke—it was a man. An *attractive* man from the sound of it. Wait a second, "attractive"? I just deleted my ex-husband's photo and I found the first man who speaks to be attractive.

I desperately needed to get out more.

I gulped, stashed my phone, and turned on the faucet.

"Just give me two more seconds!"

Be cool, he's not attractive. Be cool, he's not attractive. That became my mantra as I washed my hands.

I took a deep breath, gave one last look at myself in the mirror. Sure, I was thirty-one, but I looked better than I did in my twenties. Blonde hair, clear complexion, green eyes. I was hot.

Christine, what are you doing?!

"Nothing," I told myself quietly.

My cheeks burned as I casted my gaze downwards and opened the door, nearly running smack into a hard chest. I stumbled backwards and finally looked at the guy that was waiting by the door.

He looked like I'd startled him as well. "I'm sorry." He looked confused at his statement.

"It's open," I told him, stepping aside.

He nodded and tipped the brim of his hat to me before he ducked into the bathroom, shutting the door behind him. The click of the lock confirmed that he'd barricaded himself in there.

I stared at it for a few seconds, before I turned away, bewildered, wondering why I'd been struck dumb by an attractive man. He had the look of a man who grew up in the country and lived and breathed the great outdoors. He'd been wearing what looked like a forest ranger's uniform, and with his height, about six and a half feet tall, he looked good.

Completely unlike the wiry, slim city slickers I usually

found attractive. So why this now?

He smelled of cinnamon and pine, which made my head spin. *Spinning head and car sickness.* That was why I was fretting like this. I was just out of sorts. That's all.

My mind made up, I walked out to the main area of the mini mart and checked the fridge where the attendant had said I would find the Gatorade. I smirked to myself as I grabbed a large, cold bottle.

The good news was that I no longer felt carsick. I felt something else.

"Did you see that?"

I looked up to see Sara leaning conspiratorially into me. "See what?" I asked.

"*Him?*" She thumbed her way towards the bathroom. "Mr. Smokey Bear?"

I scoffed at her nickname. "Yeah, I did." Although it bothered me that she found him attractive too. "And I think it's Smokey *the* Bear."

"I should go camping more often," she mused.

"I'm surprised you're going camping at all," I told her.

Her face darkened. "I had to get out of Atlanta for a bit," she said.

"I know what you mean," I told her.

"No," she insisted. "I mean I *had* to get out of Atlanta."

It took a few seconds for her words to sink in. "Why?" I asked, my voice low and dangerous.

She averted her eyes.

"*Sara,*" I sighed. "What kind of trouble have you

gotten yourself into now?"

She was working at a PR Firm. She had a steady income. She was volunteering. She was doing things. Why had she fallen back on her old habits? Back in high school and college, she had gotten in with the wrong crowd and made some terrible choices. I made different ones, but she never quite grew out of hers.

So why did she drag me into this?

Furthermore, why didn't I ask the right questions when I agreed to go on this trip?

"Christine," she whispered, "I will tell you later. I'd never do anything to put you in harm's way. Just don't tell—"

The door chimed, cutting off her words. We both turned to see Emily standing in the doorway, her hands on her hips. "Are we getting back on the road or what?" she asked.

With her back to Emily, Sara pleaded with her eyes for me to not push the issue. I fought the urge to frown before I sighed and pasted on my smile, the one I keep for when I'm not feeling well but I have to do a performance.

"Yeah, I just need to buy this," I said, waving the bottle.

Emily nodded and closed the door. Through the bars on the windows, I saw her approach the Jeep where Andrea was leaning against the car.

"You're telling me as soon as we get another moment alone," I told Sara. I made sure that my tone was as unhappy as I felt. "Otherwise, you're driving me back to the airport now."

Sara nodded, which I took for her being all right with my ultimatum. "I'll get the car started. Can you get this?" She shoved a bottled frappuccino into my hands, which I had totally forgotten about between the bathroom, the park ranger, and her confession.

I shook my head as I walked up to the counter. Seriously, I couldn't believe that Sara would do this to herself again. I remembered all of the times I had to get her out of trouble. And then there were times when I couldn't get her out of trouble, because I was in trouble myself.

Some people never change.

I put the drink bottles on the counter.

"Will this be all?" the attendant, Connie Sue, asked brightly.

"Yes, thank you," I said, digging in my purse for my wallet.

A big hand slapped a five-dollar bill on the counter. "I've got this." I looked up to see Smokey Bear next to me, his eyes straight ahead. He grabbed a peppermint patty and held it up. "And this, too," he added gruffly.

I raised an eyebrow. The big guy just winked at me. The audacity.

"That'll be $4.79, Officer Donnelly," the attendant said, her smile spreading across her face. The ranger must come through here a lot. The register binged as she took out the change and deposited it in his hands. As their fingertips touched, I could see the blush on her cheek deepen.

Apparently, Smokey Bear has this effect on a lot of women.

I picked up the Gatorade and bottled coffee. "Thank you," I said, confused.

He shrugged as we turned away. "Least I could do."

"For what?"

"A pretty lady."

"Is this your way of flirting?"

A lopsided smile spread across his face. "Something like that."

He opened the door and gestured for me to go ahead.

"It may be wasted," I told him as I stepped outside. "I'm only here for a few days."

"Being nice to a pretty lady is never wasted," he said. Southern hospitality at its finest. "So you're here for camping?"

"Yeah. Up off the Chattooga River. We're staying at my friend's cabin." She wasn't technically *my* friend, but you don't go into that kind of detail when you're chit-chatting with a hot park ranger.

"The McMillan Cabin?"

"I have no idea," I said truthfully. "Do cabins have names out here?" Like they did in movies?

"Some do," he said good-naturedly. "The nice ones do. Any special reason?"

Sara's words and worry flitted through my mind, but I managed to keep my expression the same. "We just wanted a nice, relaxing vacation."

"Oh, you'll get relaxing out there," he said. He pulled out his wallet and handed me a business card. *Colton Donnelly, Park Ranger.* And there was phone number underneath it.

"What's this?" I asked.

"Just call me if there's anything you need."

"I don't get cellphone reception up here."

He pressed his lips into a fine line, and I marveled at how it accentuated his jawline. "That's a problem out here. Lack of reception for some carriers. Just keep an eye out. There lots of things to watch out for."

"Lots of mountain lions?" I joked.

"And wolves," he added. "But if you ever find yourself with cell phone coverage and want to talk or have a drink…" His voice trailed off and he grinned.

"Like a date?" I asked. I was born and raised in the city. I had no idea how you would even date out here.

"Yes, Miss…?" He paused and frowned. "Please tell me it's just 'Miss'."

I laughed. "*Miss* Christine Driver," I said, using my maiden name, even though I hadn't legally changed it yet. Yeah, yeah, I know. I just didn't do it for the longest time, and now it feels pointless.

"Colton Donnelly," he said, holding out his hand for me to shake. I took it.

"Nice to meet you. Well," I said, "I should get going. We have another forty-five minutes or so." According to GPS, most of that wasn't on a paved road, so it was going to be interesting to see how my car sickness handled it.

"Likewise," he said. "Just be careful out there, all right?" He tipped his hat to me again.

"Will do."

I took that opportunity to jog back to the Jeep where Andrea let out a low whistle.

"Look at Christine, flirting with the locals," she jokingly catcalled.

I couldn't help the grin that was spreading across my face as I settled into the passenger's seat. "He was nice. Do you know him?"

Andrea frowned. "You don't forget a face like that."

Sara watched me with an amused expression as she put the Jeep into gear. "Christine always goes native wherever she is. Whether it's mermaids or in Vegas."

I looked out the window to see Officer Donnelly get into a huge F-350 with "Georgia State Park Ranger" on the side. The big truck fit him like a glove.

Well, that was an unexpected turn of events on this vacation. And for the first time, I'd forgotten all about my worries for the mermaids.

CHAPTER 4

"OH, HOW PRETTY!" SARA EXCLAIMED AS SHE slammed the door behind her. "Andrea, I was expecting something rustic, but this is…"

"Awe-inspiring?" I finished for her, getting out of the Jeep myself.

"Yeah, that," Sara agreed.

"It's been in my family for a long time," Andrea said, crossing her arms. "I try to come out here at least once a year."

The cabin was nowhere near as rough as I'd imagined it to be. It was made out of wood, sure, but this was a two-story structure complete with a stonework chimney and green metal roof. There was even a deck that overlooked the river with a grill on it.

I'd been expecting something more in the vein of *Evil Dead*. But this was…*amazing*.

Emily was frowning behind her sunglasses. I almost thought she didn't like what she saw, but then the corner of her mouth turned up. "This is pretty awesome."

"It really is, isn't it?" Andrea said, almost proudly. "It used to be a lot worse when I was younger, but my brother renovated it about five summers ago. We even have running water now."

It certainly reinforced the phrase "glamping" in my head. Even with Sara's troubles, I was glad that I decided to come out here.

Despite everything, this was going to be a good vacation. I was sure of it.

***

Andrea flicked the lights on, illuminating the great room. Two large couches faced an entire wall of glass that looked out over the ridge and the river. A grand fireplace dominated one wall while the open concept kitchen was on the opposite end.

Fridge, stove, deck, cloudlike couches—this place was paradise.

"Why would you ever go back to Atlanta?" Sara asked Andrea, echoing my sentiments.

"I wonder that myself," Andrea said with a shrug. "Every time. But we rent it out and it helps pay for those renovations. Not a bad gig at all. Besides, my life is back in Atlanta."

I didn't know why her life wasn't here. I felt like I could truly relax here. Well, except for Sara's situation.

"There are five bedrooms," Andrea said. "And a basement. And…well, you just hang out here. We don't get internet or TV or good cell reception. So you just unplug from society for a while."

"I love it," Emily sighed. She got a mischievous grin. "Should we crack open the first bottle of wine?"

"Wine opener's in that drawer," Andrea said, pointing to the drawer on the far left. "Glasses are in the cabinet."

I helped Sara put the food away in the fridge as Emily uncorked the bottle of merlot.

"Looks like we'll get plenty of time to talk about what's going on with you while we're out here," I said to her under my breath.

Sara got a panicked look as she glanced back at Emily and Andrea, who were chatting away to themselves. "Can't we just have fun?"

"You said you'd tell me."

"But you won't believe me," she said.

I frowned. "Try me. And I can't help you if I don't know what's happening."

Our eyes met, and I held her gaze, willing her to speak. Finally, she nodded.

"Okay."

"I think the wine is going to go quickly, ladies," Emily called. She waved the empty bottle and I saw that there were four full glasses of wine. "We're already down one."

"I brought a whole case," Sara said, settling back into her carefree smile like liquid. I was actually amazed at how easily she did that. "We should be fine for four days."

She got up from her crouch in front of the fridge and walked over to the counter and picked up one of the glasses. I did the same.

"To some much-needed R-and-R," Andrea announced.

We clinked our glasses together.

***

I honestly couldn't remember the last time I sat down and read for longer than fifteen minutes. When I was in my teens, I used to sit down and read a book a day, but when I got older, I stopped reading and got caught up with life.

I found that here, life caught up with you.

I sat on the deck in an Adirondack chair, a glass of wine to my left with my paperback copy of *First Comes Love* in my hands. I was almost done with it, and I only had one more paperback to read before I was out of reading material.

Too bad I couldn't charge up my phone and download more books to read. I guess I'd have to pace myself.

The full moon hung lazily over the mountaintops. The bluish white of it reflected off the ripples on the Chattooga River. Somewhere off the distance an owl hooted, but other than that, it was a quiet, still night.

Dinner had been grilled chicken wings and vegetables, which was delicious. To my utter delight, Emily and Andrea and I were hitting it off very well, so the four of us made quite the group. I'd been worried about not fitting in with Sara's friends, but it seemed like we'd been doing great.

I checked the time on my otherwise worthless phone.

10:05pm. I wondered if everyone was in bed. Or if I could find Sara and ask her what's up.

"It's pretty, isn't it?"

I looked up to see Andrea standing in the doorway. This was the first time she and I were able to talk alone, *mano a mano.*

I grinned at her. "I agree with Sara—why would you ever go back to Atlanta? When you have all this?"

She chuckled and took another chair next to mine. "I suppose I could get satellite internet and work freelance for a few clients to make a living. But…" She sighed. "I think I would die without a Thai restaurant nearby. Or a mall."

I laughed. "Yeah, that is one of the drawbacks."

"Plus, my boyfriend works in Atlanta, so that would put a damper on things."

"That it would. Long distance is hard." Not that I'd ever had the chance to really experience it myself. Shane had been overbearing, making me feel claustrophobic. Long distance never figured into our relationship.

"Is there anyone special for you?" Andrea asked. "Back in…?"

"Jacksonville?" I finished for her. "Nah. I used to be married, but that ended."

"Oh," she said with a frown.

"It was a good thing," I corrected her. "I got out of a bad situation."

"Makes me appreciate Reggie all the more," Andrea

said after a time. "You have to hold onto the good ones."

"Yeah, you do."

"Officer Donnelly sure took an interest in you," she said playfully.

"So you know him?" I asked with a grin.

"Oh yeah," she said, stretching in her chair. "Big guy. Doesn't talk too much."

"He seemed nice."

"And hot," Sara added, diverting both of our attention to her as she came out on the deck. "Mind if I join you?"

"Not at all," I said, taking another sip of wine.

She shut the sliding door behind her and looked out over the railing. "Emily already conked out. I think she had too much."

Andrea chuckled. "She can NOT pace herself."

"My case won't last at this rate," Sara said in a mock-mournful tone.

"Neither will my books," I said, holding the paperback up.

"Hey," Andrea said, "we're here to relax. No worrying about running out of stuff. We really *are* only about forty minutes from civilization. We'll be fine."

"Yeah," Sara said distractedly. "Yeah, we will be fine."

Her words hung in the air, and I wondered if Andrea picked up the melancholy in them. I watched my sister, and now that I was paying attention, I could see the lines of worry in her face, how she masked everything with her boisterous personality.

I realized then how much I had missed her over the years. I missed how a lot of things were in the past.

Finally, after what seemed to be an eternity, Andrea stretched and yawned. "Well," she said. "At the risk of sounding like an old grandma, I think I'm going to go to bed. After all, I'm supposed to relax, right?"

I nodded, glad that this could be my moment alone with Sara. "Yep."

Andrea got up from her chair while stifling another yawn. "I'll see you guys in the morning," she said.

"Night!" I called after her.

"Good night," Sara said softly.

When the sliding door locked, I turned my gaze onto Sara and watched her, waiting for her to bring up her story. I wanted her to be the one who talked first, if only because I didn't want to prod her too much if she was traumatized by whatever this was.

But if she was going to try to weasel her way out of talking to me, she had another thing coming.

"Wow," she murmured softly. "Look at that full moon."

I picked up a note of fear in her voice. "Yeah," I said cautiously. "It's beautiful."

"I used to think so." Sara turned around and looked back at me. Her eyes were wide with fright and the rigidity told me something else was going on with her.

Finally, my patience snapped.

"Sara, what's wrong?"

"You won't believe me," she repeated, using the same

phrase she used when we were putting food away.

I crossed my arms. "I think you'll be surprised."

Sara's jaw worked. "I think I'm going to need more wine for this."

I held up my glass. "Just drink mine." *Don't think I'm letting you back in the kitchen that easily.* She'd run away and hide and hoped I'd forget about it. She wanted to talk about it, but she was too afraid to.

She took my glass and downed the rest of it in one chug. I raised my eyebrows in surprise.

"Okay," she said, as if warming herself up for our talk. "Okay."

"It will be all right," I told her.

"No, it won't." Tears started filling her eyes. "Christine, do you believe in werewolves?"

CHAPTER 5

"WEREWOLVES?" I ASKED INCREDULOUSLY. "AS in, real life werewolves?"

"See? I told you that you wouldn't believe me," Sara groaned. She put her head in her hands and started to cry.

"Yeah, yeah, I do," I said gently. I put a hand on her shoulder, but she shrugged it off, angrily.

"I mean, werewolves are supposed to just be in movies," Sara said. "Like in those horrible late night b-movies. They're not supposed to be real!"

"Just tell me what happened," I said firmly. Maybe I could get to the bottom of what she was talking about.

"Okay," Sara said. But then her face crumpled and she started crying again.

Whatever it was, it must have been terrible.

"So, I met this guy named Chad," Sara said. "At a bar in Decatur."

I didn't know anything about Atlanta's geography, but I nodded just to keep her talking.

"And we really hit it off, you know? He was nice and handsome, and everything I was looking for in a boyfriend. He took me out to dinner, we had a couple of dates. I thought, 'Wow, I found the last gentleman on Earth, and he's all mine.'"

Sounded a lot like what happened between Shane and me. I clenched my jaw.

"Go on," I prompted.

"We'd been dating for about five months," she said.

"So it's pretty serious?" I asked.

"Was," she corrected softly. "For our five-month anniversary—because Chad is so romantic—he wanted to take me out on the town. During a full moon. I should have known."

I didn't agree that a full moon would have told her that something was off, but I gently pushed her with, "What?"

She let out a breath. "He took me to dinner, where he told me that he wanted to move our relationship to the next level. And I stupidly agreed, because you know, I fall hard for any man that comes my way. I thought he meant moving in together."

She did have a habit of falling hard. I'd witnessed it firsthand. It had burned her so many times in the past too, I'd hoped that she would have learned her lesson by now.

As I said, some people never change.

Sara continued. "So I accepted, not really knowing what he meant by 'the next level'. And he said that he wanted to introduce me to his family and friends. THAT NIGHT."

"Weird."

She glared at me. "More than that. But I went with him to see his family and friends, because, 'Oh this is a romantic little surprise. He really loves me.'" She scoffed and combed a hand through her hair. "I was so wrong."

I didn't interrupt her; I let her keep talking.

"So we go over to this bar. It's in…well, it's in a rough part of Atlanta. And then I meet his friends and family—and they transformed before my very eyes."

"Transformed?"

"Into werewolves!" she cried. "They transformed into these big furry *things* and Chad tells me—just before he transforms too!—that we're going to be mated for life. And then he bites me."

I froze. "He bit you?"

"Yeah."

She reached up and pulled down the neck of her shirt down to her shoulder. Underneath was a long, scabbed bite mark that looked like it came from something inhuman with sharp teeth. It looked to be about a month old, but then again, I wasn't a doctor or anything.

"Sara, why didn't you get this stitched up?" I asked. "It could be rabies—or—"

"It's werewolves!" she cried. "See, you don't believe me, Christine!"

I swallowed back my retort, because if I argued with her anymore, she was going to shut up and not tell me her story. I needed her to calm down long enough to tell me.

"He bit me and told me that I was going to turn into a werewolf. And he wanted me to be his mate for life at the initiation during the next full moon."

I fought the urge to glance at the sky, where the full moon was watching us. "You look pretty human to me. It's a full moon now, and the only thing that's wrong is that you're crying."

She nodded. "He said that I'd have to…complete the transformation with him. That he'd find me and make me his mate."

"What does that mean?"

"I don't know! I'm not a werewolf!"

"Okay, okay. So that's why you wanted to get away from Atlanta?"

"Uh huh." She licked her lips. "I tried breaking up with him, but he refused. And then threatened me and—"

"Did you call the police?"

She gave me a hard look. "You know what it's like, being in a relationship with someone you're afraid of."

That felt like a punch to the gut, and I had to take a deep breath to steady myself as the world tilted underneath me. "Are you feeling okay?"

Her bottom lip trembled. "I think so? I don't feel any different."

"Have you talked to anyone else about this?"

"Who would I talk to?" she asked.

Good point. "So you left Atlanta during a full moon. Does he know you're here?"

She shook her head. "No."

I nodded. "Good. Okay." I put my hands on her shoulders and looked her in the eyes. "Look at me, Sara.

You're going to be fine. We have three more days to figure this out. You can move in with me in Jacksonville. You can go the police. Anything. You can get yourself out of this."

Tears filled her eyes and she hugged me, tightly. "Thank you," she whispered into my chest. "Thank you so much, Christine. I can always depend on you."

I held her and let her cry.

And I watched the moon, as if it were mocking us.

I could tell it was.

***

It was sometime after midnight before Sara was able to fall asleep. After we left the deck, I tucked her in like a little child and told her that everything was going to be all right. Eventually, her tears subsided and then became light snores.

And I was the only one awake in the house.

I stood outside, watching the full moon flit in and out of cloud cover. I kept turning Officer Donnelly's business card over and over in my hands. Debating on if I should take the Jeep and drive until I got cell phone reception to call him. Or to check the others' phones to see if they had more luck than me. Sara might be mad in the morning once she found out that I called the cops, but I couldn't stand by when someone had threatened my sister.

And if there was one thing I couldn't stand, it was someone in a position of trust threatening those I loved.

I had a breaking point when it came to people being jerk offs, and I just found it.

Officer Colton Donnelly, Park Ranger.

My mind kept mulling his name over in my head, as if I could send the distress call via telepathy.

I wondered if the other two women here knew about her situation, but I doubted it. Sara put on a brave face for everything. If there was an asteroid about to decimate Earth, she'd throw a baseball party and just pray that someone else would hit that hunk of rock back out to space.

"You think I'd be better about dealing with this kind of stuff," I groaned out loud, putting my face in my hands.

And I should.

I'd been in Sara's predicament before, and I knew how hard it was to pull myself out of that hole. How scary everything was.

I met Shane during my freshman year at the University of Jacksonville. I studied ballet and he was in school after he spent four years in the Army. We shared a huge lecture class together and I kept noticing the "hot guy" in his uniform all the time. I went and stalked Facebook until I finally found him, and even then, it took another friend messaging him to get us to start talking.

And talk we did. At first through instant messaging and then with a cup of coffee.

That first cup of coffee with him lasted three hours, and we would have kept talking if we hadn't gotten kicked out at closing.

I fell for him. And hard.

I started spending every waking moment with him. We were inseparable; you'd never see one of us without the other. My dancing suffered because of it, but hey, I was a stupid kid in love. There are worse crimes in life, but I still paid for it.

When Shane was shipped off to Iraq, I fell despondent. For two years, my identity had been with him and when he wasn't there, I no longer had any idea who I was. I stopped going to class. I stopped caring.

I dropped out of college waiting for him. I took a job at a restaurant to pay for my living wages. And when he came back, I still waited for him. Because the man who came back wasn't the same Shane that left. This was a battle-hardened man that I barely knew. Sure, I said yes when he asked me to marry him. We got married too early. We moved in together too early.

At first, I'd convinced myself that this was all right. That this was how love should be and love had rough patches. I worked at the restaurant while he took a job at the bar in a seedy part of Jacksonville. We were getting by, albeit, we weren't together most of the time.

I think that was when we started drifting apart.

And that was when the hitting started. The screaming. The accusing glares.

I hid the bruises under my heavy waterproof makeup. I blamed myself for what my fledgling marriage had become.

The man who was now Shane was a different kind of beast from the one I originally fell in love with.

And I would do anything I could to repair it. Unfortunately, he took me up on my offer to do that.

A howl rent through the night, making me snap my head up, crashing through my memories of the past.

Was that a wolf? It sounded a bit too close for my liking, but then again, we were out in the wilderness of Georgia, and Officer Donnelly had said to look out for wolves. I guess they were close by no matter where we were out here.

That solidified my decision that I was not going to go out in the Jeep and find cell reception, especially in unfamiliar woods.

I thought about what Sara had said about werewolves, and I wondered for a brief second if that was a werewolf indeed. There was a full moon, after all.

Did I believe her story about werewolves? Sure. But that's because I've seen a lot of things in my lifetime, from a baby dolphin jumping an impossible distance to things like—

Another howl. This one much closer, followed by an answer.

I shivered and pulled my cardigan closer around me, even though the summer air was hot and humid. I forgot how true fear can make your insides turn to ice.

Maybe it was time to go inside.

I opened the sliding door and stepped into the

darkened great room. I locked it, and pulled the curtain shut, blocking out the full moon. What was out there could stay out there, and I was going to sleep in here, safe and sound.

Scrrraaaaa—tch.

The sound echoed throughout the cabin, and I froze in place, hearing the pounding of my heartbeat in my ears.

It's just the wind, Christine. A tree branch or something scratching on the window.

I wished I could convince my nerves of that. There weren't any trees close enough to do that.

I jumped as I heard something big hit the roof with a thud, and then scuttle along one side of it.

I couldn't convince myself that it was the wind this time.

And then I heard the screaming.

CHAPTER 6

"CHRISTINE!"

Sara was screaming my name, spurring me into motion. I glanced around, trying to find a weapon, anything that could do damage to an assailant. I wished Andrea's family were hunters, but I couldn't see any sign of guns.

A kitchen knife would have to do. I practically tore the drawer off its track and jostled the cutlery. I pulled out the biggest knife I could find, which was still woefully small for whatever was attacking us.

A loud crash brought me to a run. It sounded like a window upstairs, in Sara's bedroom.

I ran towards it, hoping that I wouldn't get there to see my sister torn to pieces or—

Halfway up the stairs, I ran smack into her. Luckily, not with the pointy end of my knife.

"Christine!" she cried. Her eyes were wild and her fingers dug into my upper arm. "They're here! They're here!"

"Who's here?" I asked, although I knew the answer.

"Chad. And—"

Another crash, followed by another scream. Emily, it

sounded like.

"Look," I told Sara, taking charge of the situation. "Go down to the basement."

"Don't leave me!"

"Sara!" I shook her shoulder. "Trust me on this, okay?"

She was white as a sheet, but she nodded. "Basement?" she whimpered.

"Hurry, and don't open the door until you hear me on the other side, okay?"

"'K."

I knew what they said about splitting up. But with the way that Sara looked right now, she'd get herself hurt and me as well. As big of a risk as it was, she had to hole herself up somewhere safe. I just hoped that safe place was downstairs.

"Go," I told her. She bounded down the stairs as I went up. Towards danger. Towards the unknown.

Both of which were terrifying.

I held the knife in front of me, ready to slash anything that pounced on me.

Should I call out Emily or Andrea's name? Let them know I'm coming? Or should I stay silent?

I opted for the latter and reached the landing as quietly as possible. Sara's bedroom door was wide open. I didn't dare look inside. I just had to make sure that Emily and Andrea were safe.

The door to the room where Emily was staying was slightly ajar. My breathing was quick as I pushed it open and peered in.

At first, I saw nothing. Then I saw Emily in a heap on the floor with a huge, hulking figure standing over her, its back to me. At first, I couldn't quite identify what it was. While it was on all four legs, it felt like it took up most of the room. A grey wolf.

My ears picked up the sound of it sniffing the air, like it knew I was there.

Then it turned towards me, and I saw the red, bloodshot eyes.

I screamed as it howled at me.

But then I surprised it. Instead of cowering in fear or running, I charged it, brandishing the knife (which, I knew for certain, was way too small for this monster) like a madwoman and aimed to plunge it into its chest. I'm no knife expert, but I stuck it somewhere.

The knife pierced the beast in its side, and it threw back its head and screamed. Before I could react, it scrambled on all fours and leapt out the window.

Leaving me with an unconscious Emily.

One look at her, and I knew that she was just knocked out cold with no permanent damage, except maybe a conk on her pretty head, but it would have been much worse if I arrived later. I bent down and heaved her arm around my shoulder and practically dragged her out of the bedroom.

Was that the only werewolf in here? Were there more?

I knew for certain now that there were indeed werewolves after Sara. As much as it was terrifying, it also broke my heart to know that my sister was entangled with such creatures.

Maybe I got the only one that attacked us?

Better to be safe than sorry.

So, Andrea's room it was. I pulled Emily alongside me as I crossed the landing to Andrea's room. Unlike the other two doors, this one was closed. Hopefully that meant she was safe.

I banged on it three times, before trying the doorknob. Thankfully, it was unlocked and it opened easily. In the dark room, nothing seemed like it was out of place, except for Andrea sitting bolt upright in bed.

"What the—?" she started, angry at my intrusion.

"Get to the basement." I turned on the light, blinding both of us. "*Now.*"

She opened her mouth, but then saw me supporting a limp Emily. Before she could ask what happened, another thud hit the roof, much closer now that I was on the top level. We both jumped at the noise, and Andrea let out a little shriek.

Wordlessly, she got to her feet, although her breathing was shallow. She would hyperventilate if she didn't get herself under control. *Keep it together.*

I followed her out of the room.

"Sara?" she asked as she looked at the open doorway to where my sister had been sleeping.

"She's already downstairs," I told her. "C'mon."

Between the two of us, we somehow got ourselves and

Emily's unconscious body down two flights of stairs. When we reached the basement level, I saw that it was closed and locked to my relief.

Good girl, I told Sara silently.

I pounded on this door. "Sara, it's me!"

There was a pause followed by the sound of the lock being turned. As if it would protect her, she cracked the door open to confirm that it was just us. Our eyes locked and she threw open the door with a sob.

"Oh, thank god!"

I didn't have time to hug her or tell her that everything was all right. I shuffled inside, bringing Emily with me.

"What happened to her?" Sara cried, her hands covering her mouth. Andrea shut the door behind us, locked it, and put a chair under the handle. We'd all seen enough movies to know the drill during a home invasion.

"She's just unconscious," I said. "She'll be fine."

I'd been in the basement earlier today, but I hadn't spent much time here. There was just a couch on which I laid Emily, a coffee table, a television with a shelf of DVDs next to it, a small fridge, and a cabinet with some drawers. Maybe something could be used as a weapon, but not against odds like this.

"What the hell is happening?" Andrea hissed. Her eyes were wide like Sara's.

"We have intruders," I said, not willing to get into the details of werewolves.

"Did you see one?" Sara asked.

I knew exactly what she meant. I nodded.

A long, ragged scraping noise split through our conversation. This time, it didn't sound like it was on the outside of the house.

It was directly above us, like claws were being dragged across the floor.

Sara covered up her shriek as she looked up, her eyes following the noise. Andrea jumped and moved to the corner. Her eyes were up on the ceiling as well.

The long scrape was joined by another and another and another. Like an entire pack was standing in the great room above.

Werewolves.

They weren't going to leave. As much as I didn't want to, I had to do something. I'd lost my knife earlier and I certainly wasn't going to get anything down here with which to fight back. I had to show my true colors.

I swallowed back the lump in my throat. "I'll be back."

Sara snapped her gaze to me. "WHAT?"

I gave her a grim smile. "I'm going to show them that they can't just come in here."

Andrea shook her head, slowly at first, then violently. Sara looked like she couldn't believe what I was saying.

"No, Christine! NO!"

"I promise," I told her, "I will be right back. When have I ever let you down?"

She looked dubious, which was a welcome sight compared to her fear.

"Just lock this door behind me and put as much furniture as you can in front of the door." I didn't mention that the werewolves above could tear through the floor in a heartbeat and get them. Like shooting fish in a barrel.

Before they could protest anymore, I pulled out the chair and opened the door, slowly at first to see if there was anything in the stairwell.

There wasn't.

"I'll be back," I promised one more.

"Be careful, Christine," Sara said.

"Hey," I told her. "I'm your big sister. I'll take care of this."

Before I could hear her response, I shut the door behind me.

It was just me and them now.

CHAPTER 7

NOW THAT I WAS ALONE, I NEEDED TO ACT quickly.

"It had to be wolves," I muttered under my breath.

I quickly stripped off my dress, bra, and panties and stowed them down at the bottom of the stairs, right next to the door. It wouldn't do to rip one of the four outfits I had here. I was wearing my favorite dress after all. Still, I wasn't a nudist, so being naked made me feel exposed.

I closed my eyes and called to my inner beast.

It had been forever since I transformed. Luckily, my cycles weren't dictated by the full moon like werewolves were, so l hadn't had to do it in a very long time.

Here's to hoping that I wasn't rusty. I was frankly dreading the sensation, like I always did.

I felt the fur start sprouting down my spine and then spreading across my back. I fell to my hands and knees as the transformation changed the physiology of my feet. Bones rearranged and shifted. I felt my skin and tendons moving and stretching to accommodate this new form. My mouth pulled forward and widened as whiskers poked their way through my upper lip. My ears shifted to the top of my head. The shape of my eyes changed, and how I saw the world changed too.

I *became* a mountain lion.

When I said that I'd do anything to repair my relationship with Shane, I meant it. The actual way in which he brought up to me that he had become a mountain lion shifter is fuzzy—something about becoming friends with the guys at the bar and how they showed him a whole new world—but he had issued an ultimatum that I join him in this crazy, messed-up society of werecats or he'd leave me. He'd been the one who transformed me. It was a decision I've regretted every day since.

I closed my eyes in mourning for my lost humanity.

No time to think on the past; I had werewolves to kick out.

With liquid, stealthy steps, I moved up the stairs, ready to spring forward at any moment if there was so much as a creak that sounded out of place.

I was a big cat. I stood at about waist high and I weighed about the same as when human, which, when you're talking about an animal, is pretty frightening. Still though, I wasn't sure how I'd compare with grey wolves. At least I had the element of surprise working for me. They had no idea what I was. Hopefully my unfamiliar scent would throw them off. But now that I had theirs, they had another thing coming to them.

I reached the ground floor, my keen cat-ears picking up any hint of movement. They were still in the middle of the great room, scraping their claws against the floor, as if to terrorize my friends below. It had the appropriate effect, because I'd felt that same fear downstairs.

Now, though, I was ready to teach them a lesson.

Three...two...one...

Like a tensed up coil, I sprang into action, catching the closest wolf by surprise. I didn't hesitate; I went for the throat, although I didn't want to kill him. He screeched inhumanly as my weight took him down, crashing into a wall.

I had about another heartbeat before the other werewolves realized that they had a werecat on their hands, so I tackled another one, raking my claws across his chest. Blood spurted from the wound, only feeding my natural instincts to keep fighting.

The second werewolf went down just as easily as the first. His head connected with the edge of the wooden coffee table, and it knocked him senseless. I knew that Andrea wouldn't be happy with the dent I made in the wall and the damage to her furniture, but I bet she'd be happier than the alternative.

From my right side, I was bodily thrown, hitting above the fireplace. The stonework dug into my back and scratched me painfully as I fell to the floor in a heap.

In any other ordinary situation, I would have just let the pain wash over me. It *hurt*, and every fiber of my being was screaming at me to stop, go get medical help. It had been so long since I'd been in a fight with another shifter,

I'd forgotten how much it sucked.

I forced myself to my feet though, and I bared my teeth, giving them a cry.

Five werewolves watched me, shocked for a moment before baring their teeth with an answering growl.

If we were all the same species, we could communicate with each other in our animal language. I could figure out which one was Chad—if any of them were Chad—and teach him a lesson for threatening my sister.

As it was though, we were woefully only able to speak different languages, so I couldn't pick up what they were saying to each other.

Better to keep them occupied as opposed to planning their next moves right in front of me.

I moved first, swiping at the face of the closest werewolf. My claws caught his skin, and I felt the flesh tear underneath them. That was going to leave a mark in the morning.

Without waiting to see his reaction, I lunged towards another werewolf, this one a female. She was smaller than the others and we traded blows for a few passes before my paw slapped her across the face, throwing her into the wall. She was still conscious, but backing away from me. So long as I kept an eye on her, she wasn't going to be trouble.

Three more to go.

Claws raked my back and I yowled before using my teeth to tear my assailant off me. I snapped loudly as I circled him. This one was the biggest one, the same monster I'd seen in Emily's room.

I could tell with certainty that he was the leader of the group. He just had that air about him that marked him as Alpha.

Another wolf came at me, but my paw connected with his jaw, spinning him around once before he landed in a heap.

I faced the leader and bared my teeth at him, yelling as loudly as I could in my cat-language.

"Leave! And don't you dare come back!"

There was no way that he'd be able to understand what I was saying, but he got the meaning of what I was trying to convey. His red eyes narrowed before he snapped to the other wolves in his pack. Two of them that were hurt the worst whimpered back at him, but he hissed at me.

They understood my warning.

They all got to their feet and trotted up the staircase to the second floor, to leave through the windows through which they had entered. Why leave through the door when they made such a grand entrance?

The last one, the leader, gave me the side-eye one more time before padding up the stairs.

I caught his drift though. *We'll be back with more.*

I just hoped we had enough time to regroup and figure out our next move before that happened. When I got back downstairs to the basement, I was going to order everyone to pack their bags because we were leaving.

It appeared that our vacation was going to be cut short.

A few seconds later, my ears pricked at the sound of a low hiss in the distance, followed by metal crunching.

No! Nononononono.

I ran to the front door. I controlled my transformation enough to turn my right paw into a human hand, and I unlocked and opened the door. I ran outside to the Jeep, which I saw had all of its tires punctured and losing air, quickly. We only had one spare tire. There was also a huge dent in the hood, and I knew that meant the engine was damaged somehow.

They made sure that leaving in a car wasn't an option.

Dammit!

Rustling in the distance perked my ears. Those bastards were running away. Maybe they had cars nearby and I could take one to civilization. Maybe call the police. Maybe call Officer Donnelly and join the Witness Protection program.

Except no one would believe our story.

Still, I bounded after the noise, running as fast as my four legs would carry me. I was injured and sore from the fight, but I willed myself to keep moving. On the slim chance that I could catch up with them, we could find a way out of here. I'd make sure they would listen.

I reached a clearing before I stopped. I realized that I was too far from the cabin. If these bastards got the idea that they could lead me away from the house and circle back, I just fell into their trap.

Then again, I could be wrong and letting our only lead get away.

Indecision tore at me as my painful injuries finally started sinking in. I hadn't thought I'd gotten *that* hurt from the fight, but apparently I had.

Only one way to find out how bad it was, even though I didn't want to do it. But I couldn't just show up in the basement as a werecat. Or even transform there. I was pretty sure that Sara and the others were holed up in the basement until I came back, so there was no chance of them seeing me in my birthday suit.

And I felt oh so sore after everything.

Decision made, I transformed back into a human. The fur disappeared, my face and muscle structure shifted back to being that of a woman. I rolled my head on my neck, glad that my body felt familiar again. It felt like I was sloughing off the skin of a predator and I was always glad to reconnect with my human side.

Being a werecat, you could lose that connection. I felt like myself. Exposed, but at least human. As a bonus, my scent would change and they couldn't smell a mountain lion anymore.

Unsteadily, I stood on my legs and went to my full height, wincing as my muscles and torn skin fell back into place. As a human, I was more familiar with *where* it hurt, but it didn't make it hurt any less.

My shoulder ached and the angry stings on my back indicated that I had a few good scratches. My right eye was also swelling shut.

Wonderful. It must look like I had gotten into a car

wreck. It certainly wouldn't look good for my mermaid performances for a few weeks.

"This is not the vacation I'd been hoping for," I muttered.

I stepped forward in a ginger, timid motion. At least I still had my balance and my bearings. I'd take it.

I jogged my way back to the cabin, careful not to make too much noise but also quickly as I was reasonably sure that the werewolves had had the same idea I did about circling back to the cabin. I had to hurry.

When I neared the clearing where the cabin lay about forty feet ahead of me, the sound of a twig snapping forced me to skid to a halt, my heart pounding in my ears.

At first, I didn't see or hear anything. And then, a familiar voice cried out, "Who's there?"

I covered my eyes as a flashlight shone on me, blinding me momentarily. I recovered just enough to peek around and feel the sense of dread and embarrassment hit me all at once.

Officer Donnelly. Seeing me naked in the forest. He was *here*, which meant that his huge truck wasn't too far away, our seemingly only chance of getting back to civilization alive.

I was almost relieved, when I realized that he didn't seem too flustered to see me running naked through the woods after midnight. Then I realized how odd of a coincidence it was that he'd be here at the same time of night when we were attacked by werewolves.

He's one of them.

He lowered the flashlight. "Christine, was it?" he asked, confused.

I didn't answer. I grabbed the closest rock next to me, and, without thinking about the consequences of hitting an officer of the law, I chucked it at him, aiming for his head. I was a pitcher on the softball team in high school, and while that had been over a decade ago, I still had a mean pitch.

It connected with his temple and the big man dropped like a ton of bricks.

I breathed heavily for a moment, panicking that I might have just killed the park ranger, before bending down and throwing his huge, muscular arm about my shoulders. It was the second time tonight that I was dragging someone.

I didn't know exactly what I was going to do once I got him back to the cabin. But I did know that when he woke up, he had a bunch of questions to answer.

One of them being where the heck he'd parked his truck.

CHAPTER 8

I POUNDED ON THE DOOR TO THE BASEMENT. "It's me!" I yelled, a little too gruffly. "Let me in!"

I heard a scuffle on the other side before the door inched open and Andrea's wide, frightened eyes peered at me. "Christine?" she stammered. "Are you okay? Who's that? And *why are you naked?*"

Damn.

I'd forgotten to put my clothes back on. It was amazing what adrenaline and fear could do to make you forget about everyday conveniences. Like clothes. From the moment I dropped the park ranger with a rock, my only objective was to get back to the basement and get everyone out of here.

I didn't even think about the clothes that were at my feet.

"This is Officer Donnelly," I said, nodding towards the unconscious man whose arm I had slung about my shoulders. As if that explained anything. "And I'm naked because…"

My voice trailed off because I had no idea how to finish that statement. Thankfully, the door flew open and Sara launched herself at me, sobbing big tears. I let go of the park ranger and held my sister for a second.

"Christine!" she cried. "I thought you'd—you'd…"

"I'm fine," I told her quickly. "Let's get him inside and we need to figure out where his truck is. We don't have much time."

She helped me drag him into the basement, and just before we shut the door, I grabbed my clothes. Everyone had gotten a pretty good look at me so far, but I wasn't going to spend the rest of the night without clothes on. A girl had to have priorities.

Emily was still lying on the couch, unconscious. I hoped she would be all right. But that also meant that we had two people who were otherwise unable to move at the moment.

I grabbed a roll of paper towels from the sink and started dabbing at anything that was bleeding on me. I doubted there was a first aid kit down here, so the best that I was going to be able to do was clean up my wounds. I couldn't see out of my right eye too much, but I thought it was fine.

So much for keeping my favorite dress clean.

"What's that park ranger doing here?" Andrea said.

"I think he's with them," I said as I snapped my bra into place and pulled my dress over it. "I caught him outside in the woods."

"With *who*?" Andrea demanded, at the same time Sara asked, "What were you doing out in the *woods*?"

"The werewolves," I explained quickly.

"*Werewolves?*" Andrea exclaimed.

"And I chased the werewolves out into the woods, Sara," I continued, my single-track mind moving a million miles a minute. "Andrea, do you have anything to tie him up with down here? Like rope or duct tape?"

"Werewolves?" she repeated.

"Duct tape, Andrea!"

She gave herself a visible shake. "There's duct tape in that drawer." She pointed to the cabinets. I opened it and rummaged through it. Luckily, I found an almost-complete roll of the silver tape. Perfect. I was going to use all of it to tie him up. I wasn't taking any chances.

"Christine, what's going on?" Sara asked. "How did you chase them out in the woods?"

I sat Officer Donnelly up and pulled his arms behind his back. He was so muscular, his triceps nearly got in the way of me binding his wrists. I didn't want to think about how nice and strong and attractive those arms were. Especially now.

"I think they're circling back," I said, "and—"

"*How did you chase them?*" Sara asked. She stopped. "I mean, there were lots of wolves."

"I caught them by surprise." I knew, fleetingly, that the jig was up.

Sara swallowed. "You're one of them."

I stopped wrapping the tape around the park ranger's wrists and sighed. "Not exactly," I said at length.

But it was too late. I saw the terror in Sara's face, the

betrayal that she thought that I was one of the monsters that was hunting her. It was true that I was a monster, but I wasn't one of *these* monsters. And I had to make her see that. I had to make both of them see that.

Andrea's face was pinched into the deepest frown I'd ever seen on anyone. She was mentally catching up. I just needed to head that off before either of them got any ideas. There were a few items down here that could be used as blunt weapons, and I was too tired to fight them on it.

"I'm not a werewolf, Sara," I told her evenly. "I'm a—" I hesitated, because I hadn't told anyone in years "—a mountain lion shifter."

That statement hung between us and their looks turned from suspicious to just plain confused.

"A mountain…?" Sara started, but she couldn't even say it.

"A mountain lion shifter," I finished.

Andrea shook her head and cursed under her breath. "You're crazy. You are absolutely—"

I shapeshifted my hand into a paw, obvious enough to not be a wolf paw, but not monstrous enough to freak them out even further.

"Oh my god," Sara whimpered, cowering in the corner. "How?"

"It was a big factor in why I divorced Shane," I explained. I morphed my hand back so I could continue restraining Donnelly. "He turned me into a mountain lion.

And I hated living in that world. So *this*..." I twirled my finger around, indicating this messed up situation. "...this whole thing, you don't want to be a part of it. Take it from someone who knows, and who has been running from that life for ten years. I'm going to get you out of here."

"Shane did this to you?" Sara asked, her voice broken.

I snickered. "Yeah. I told you it was a bad marriage."

I resumed duct taping Officer Donnelly up tightly. Once I had his wrists bound behind him, feet and legs bound in front of him, and a couple of times around the torso, *then* I would feel comfortable about having him down here. If he transformed, I was reasonably sure that he wouldn't be able to free himself. I didn't gag him with the tape, only because I knew that we'd have to ask him where his truck was in order to get out of here. And if he knew where the other werewolves were.

That is, if *he's with the werewolves,* my thoughts nagged at me.

Of course he was. Why else would he be out by the cabin after midnight? Also, I immensely hoped so, because otherwise, I'd be in big trouble with the law.

If that were the case though, I'd deal with that later. We had bigger things to worry about.

Like a pack of werewolves that now knew that there was a werecat among us.

Sara and Andrea watched me, all too shocked at this turn of events. It made me regret the fact that I'd never told Sara about my deepest, darkest secret. She knew that my relationship with Shane had turned sour. She just never knew how deeply it scarred me. I focused intently on my actions, hoping that I wouldn't freak them out any further by making too-quick movements.

"Ugh, what happened?"

We all looked over the couch where Emily was trying to sit up. She struggled for a bit and then winced as she laid back down. She grunted and finally put herself into a sitting position. "My head," she whimpered softly.

That was one less thing to worry about.

Andrea sat on the couch next to her and checked her head and vitals. "We were attacked," she explained softly. "How's your head?"

Emily grimaced and put her head in her hands. "Attacked?"

Andrea licked her lips, indecision on her face. "Yeah, attacked."

And as she launched into a bad recap of what happened, I turned my attention back to Sara who was still watching me like I'd bite her at any given moment.

"I never told you," I said, "because I didn't want you to think that I was crazy."

Her eyes bugged out of her head. "Crazy? *Crazy?* Here I was, worried that you didn't believe my story about werewolves, when this whole time—this *whole* time…"

I did one more wrap of tape around Officer Donnelly. He was already pretty secure, but I needed something to do with my hands. "I wasn't sure if you were on drugs or if you saw something and believed it—"

She came over and pushed me, catching me off guard and knocking me to my butt. "You!" she cried through gritted teeth. "Out of all people, *you* were doubting that?"

"I was in denial," I told her coolly. "I knew that you believed in what you saw. I just hoped that you wouldn't have the same fate I did."

She crossed her arms. "And what fate is that?"

"A lifetime in hiding. I don't know much about werewolves, but even though werecats are pretty solitary, there's a huge pecking order and you're constantly on your guard. I imagine it would be worse with werewolves. I *hoped* you didn't face that, Sara. I wanted you to have a happy ending."

Because I wasn't going to have one.

I sighed and ran my hands through my hair. I'm sure I looked like a mess. Now that the effects of my transformation and the tension had left my system, I was starting to feel my aches and pains again. I hoped my scrapes and scratches were scabbed over by now.

But I probably could consider this dress ruined.

"You could have told me," Sara said softly.

I looked up at her and my gaze softened. "I realize that now." I pushed myself to my feet. "And if we get out of here alive, I won't ever doubt you again."

The corner of her mouth turned up. "Likewise."

"So, now that we've established that werewolves are indeed real," I said, "you have to tell me if you feel the need to morph or turn into one."

She shook her head. "No, I feel fine. That was a part of it though: Chad said that I had to do something in order to make this transformation permanent. And to be *his*, forever." She shuddered.

"Is he one of the werewolves out there?" I asked.

"Yes."

I ran through each of the werewolves' faces in my mind, trying to figure out which one was Chad. "Was he the big one? Is he the alpha?"

She considered my question and then shook her head. "I don't know if he's the alpha."

I thought about my own situation with Shane and his friends before I realized what they were. There was one that he always deferred to, and while cats don't have that pack mentality that wolves do, there was an order to it. That friend was the leader of our werecat group. And he was dangerous, even more so than living with Shane.

But I didn't say that out loud. One step at a time.

"We'll get out of here," I promised her.

"Some vacation this turned out to be," she scoffed.

"I went into this knowing that nothing was ever simple with you," I said with a mischievous grin. "This is all just a part of the fun."

That last part was true, and I only realized as I said it. For the first time in *years,* I felt alive. I may have hated this aspect of my life, but at least it was interesting and kept things in perspective. It was such a strange sensation, like the werecat inside me was pacing, happy to be out of its literal cage.

"Where...am I?" a voice croaked, interrupting us.

We both turned our heads to see Officer Donnelly waking up. Just in time too. Because I was going to ask him some questions and hopefully save all of our lives.

CHAPTER 9

"WHERE AM I?" OFFICER DONNELLY REPEATED, his voice stronger now.

I stepped over towards him and looked down at him, hoping that I could intimidate the big man as best as I could. He was glaring up at me, and having a big, attractive man do that to you—angrily—is one of the most disconcerting things I've ever felt.

"You should know," I told him coolly.

"No, I do not," he replied icily.

I put my hands on my hips. "Try."

Behind me, Emily and Andrea had stopped talking to each other and had fallen silent, watching our conversation. Sara stood behind me, as if I shielded her from him.

I was the only form of protection they had.

Officer Donnelly blinked, then looked down at himself, at his restraints and sighed. "You realize that this is a Federal offense, right? And did you hit me with a rock?"

"We're not playing by the rules right now," I said. "Especially since your kind doesn't."

"And what is my kind?"

"Werewolves," Sara whispered behind me.

He waited a beat and then burst out laughing. "Werewolves?" he asked. "Seriously?"

I clenched my jaw, refusing to yield. Doubt, however, creeped into the back of my mind, whispering thoughts that I was very, very wrong and made a terrible mistake.

No, I told myself firmly. *He* has *to be one of them. Why else would he be out in the woods at this time of night?*

After everything in life, I no longer believed in coincidences.

"You were outside our cabin," I told him. "After midnight."

"I was doing my rounds," he said.

"Uh-huh," I said. "And do your rounds involve getting out of your truck and trespassing on private property?"

I didn't exactly know the law, but he'd have to have a warrant or something, right?

He only glared up at me in answer. "So what do you think I was doing?"

Sara cast a look of worry my way, but I kept my eyes on him. "I think you know what you were doing."

He shook his head with a short laugh. "No, I don't!"

"Christine," Emily said from the couch. I tried not feeding into her worry. Although I knew, that out of the four women here, I was the only one standing alone in this conviction.

"He was outside, on the property, after I chased off the werewolves!" I said, pointing at the park ranger. "You don't think that's weird?"

"No," Officer Donnelly said, "what's weird is seeing a naked woman running through the woods after midnight, and then she knocks you out and ties you up."

"Maybe we should just let him go," Emily said uncertainly.

"He's a werewolf," I insisted.

"I'll have you know that drugs are a Federal offense too," he threatened. Was he insinuating that we were on drugs? I almost laughed. "In fact, you're breaking so many laws down here…"

"I had nothing to do with this!" Andrea shouted behind me.

Emily sobbed, confused with the entire situation.

"We were attacked, Officer," Sara pleaded, stepping between us. "Pardon my sister, we've had such a bad night…"

"Sara, get back," I hissed through gritted teeth.

I spoke too late. The tape that I had thought had secured and restrained his limbs shredded as he lunged out at her from a seated position, transforming into a werewolf as he did so.

Two thoughts entered my mind. First, that my instincts were correct, he was a werewolf and he was dangerous.

Second, that I had to protect my sister.

I roughly shoved Sara behind me, transforming into my werecat form as I did so. So much for saving this dress—it tattered and shredded as my body changed and morphed. I threw myself between them, making my body as big as possible, looking as threatening as possible. The beast that was Officer Donnelly paused, taking in the sight and the fact that I was a mountain lion.

Screams filled the claustrophobic space of the basement, Sara, Emily, and Andrea. My sensitive ears picked up on it, and if I'd been human, I would have winced. As it was, I had to push their screams away from my mind.

Even in his wolf form, Donnelly looked confused at my sudden transformation. Like he hadn't been expecting it.

I wasn't falling for it. I bared my teeth and paced between them, daring him to try something, *anything*.

Instead, he stayed where he was. As if he was dumbfounded by this turn of events.

But he should have seen this coming. After all, he'd been one of the wolves from earlier. He *saw* me in the woods. He was here at a weird time, for Pete's sake. *He was a werewolf.*

Do it, I told him silently. *Fight me. I dare you.*

A pity that I was going to have to mess up his rugged, handsome face.

"Christine," Sara said, diverting my attention for just moment.

I turned so that I could keep one eye on him and one eye on my sister. She was backing up to the couch, white as a sheet. Emily and Andrea both looked like they were going to be sick at all this.

Donnelly stepped forward, and I snapped all of my

attention back to him. No way he was going to get past me.

"Ugh, fine," I heard Andrea say dimly behind me. "Forget Chad's orders. Do I have to do everything myself?" What the hell did that mean?

I didn't have time to wonder. He launched himself forward and I only had time to tense up, ready for the attack.

"CHRISTINE!" Sara screamed again. Was it in warning?

The sensation of Donnelly's teeth on my jugular never came. Instead, he brushed right past me, and I snapped at him as he passed. I wasn't his target. I had never been his target. He bounded towards the couch, towards Sara.

And I was too late to stop him.

Yet, there were no longer just humans on the couch. As I followed Donnelly's trajectory, I saw the transformation of one of them. *Andrea.* Andrea was transforming into a werewolf herself, her teeth bared to...

To get Sara.

I screeched in anger, rushing forward to intercept Andrea's attack. Donnelly got there first, barreling into Andrea, and both beasts hit the wall with a deafening thud. DVDs and trinkets fell off the shelves as they roared at each other.

What I saw was something like two dogs fighting. Despite Donnelly's size as a human, Andrea made a formidable opponent against him. Their teeth snapped at each other, their claws raking deep wounds into shoulders and chests. Yelping, barking, growling filled the air in quick succession.

It was a fight to the death.

All Sara and Emily could do was watch in horror. Hell, all *I* could do was watch in horror. What do you do when a supposed friend was actually a monster, and she was fighting the monster that you knew was a park ranger too? Was Emily one too? Or would Sara turn into one?

What the hell was this?

I was getting so confused at this turn of events.

I jumped to the other side of the couch, keeping myself between the fighting monsters. Sara watched them, her jaw on the floor, while Emily sobbed in terror.

What should I do? What *could* I do?

The two beasts broke apart, panting from exertion and their injuries. I was hurt badly earlier, but these two were bleeding and spitting out blood. Donnelly was missing part of his ear while Andrea had deep scratches.

I heard a noise that I didn't recognize at first, and then I realized with horror that it was laughing through a strangled throat. Andrea was laughing.

She looked my way and gave a smirk. There was something sinister in that smirk. Like a promise to return. Or worse.

Then she pushed her way past me at a speed I hadn't expected. She tore across the room, and when she got to the door, she didn't stop. She hit it full on with her shoulders, blowing the door off its hinges.

She went up the stairs, out of sight, leaving a werecat, a werewolf, and two other people whom I assumed were still human. Although nothing would have surprised me tonight.

But it seemed the danger was gone. At least for now.

Donnelly and I looked at each other and he nodded slightly.

I nodded in return. *Truce.*

I quietly called back my inner beast and transformed back into a human. Donnelly did the same, cradling his torn, bloodied ear. We were going to have to figure out what just happened.

Emily broke the sudden quiet with a scream: "IS EVERYONE HERE A WEREWOLF?"

CHAPTER 10

THERE WERE NO CLOTHES IN THE CABIN BIG enough to really fit Donnelly after he transformed back into a human. Thankfully, he had pants that still somewhat functioned, much like the Hulk's pants. I was able to find one of my nightshirts that covered up much of his chest, although it was tight across his biceps.

There was something rather funny about seeing a grown man wearing a pink shirt that said, "Lewisburg High School 2003 Girl's Softball Team."

"Thanks," he said, rolling the shirt down over his abs.

"Don't mention it," I said, feeling my cheeks flush with embarrassment.

On the other hand, my dress wasn't as lucky as his pants. The poor thing was done for and when I had transformed back, I was once again naked. I went upstairs by myself and dragged my rolling bag back downstairs to change.

All semblance of modesty was gone for me tonight. If I lived through this, I was never going to live it down.

One thing was certain though: with the door torn off the hinges, the basement was wide open and we'd have to keep moving.

"So let me get this straight," Emily said as I tied my sneakers. Her voice pitched an octave higher than normal as she spoke. "There's a group of werewolves that's after Sara. Andrea is one of them and probably ratted us out to them. Hell, even offered her cabin as bait. Ranger Rick here is a werewolf, but he's not a part of that group of werewolves. Christine is a mountain lion. And I'm just here because I wanted to go on vacation?"

"That's why I'm here too," I reminded her.

She shook her head. "How am I supposed to believe that?"

"Because it's the truth." I finished double-knotting my shoelaces and got to my feet. Hopefully I wasn't going to have to transform any more tonight. These were my favorite pair of running sneakers and it would be devastating if I had to ruin them too.

"I should have stayed home," Emily muttered, putting her face in her hands.

I didn't want to point out to her that this was all kind of Sara's fault. If she had told me about her predicament before we left Atlanta, we would have been able to figure this whole thing out. As it was, well, this wasn't going to be the restful vacation that I hoped for.

"If you weren't a part of the werewolf pack from earlier," I said, look at Donnelly, "what were you doing out in the woods?"

He sighed and ran his fingers through his hair. "I heard them howling to each other." He gave me a hard look.

"You don't hear werewolves like that unless they're moving to attack someone. So I came to investigate."

"As a park ranger or as a werewolf?" I asked.

"Does it matter?" he asked.

"I need to know if I have to stay on the right side of the law tonight," I told him. "I need to know if you're here as Officer Donnelly or as a werewolf."

He chuckled. "Touché. I'm here as a friend. I knew you all were out here, and I was worried about you."

That made my stomach twist in a funny way, and I swallowed, hard.

"Okay," I said.

He rubbed the back of his neck. "And then you knocked me out."

"The bigger they are, the harder they fall."

He sneered. "With a rock."

"Sorry about that." Apparently, I wasn't very good with an action-movie kind of bravado.

But he smiled and said, "I probably would have done the same thing in your position."

Our eyes connected. When was the last time I'd seen eyes so blue? And again, there were butterflies flitting about in my stomach, distracting my thoughts. I needed to stop this and get my head back in the game.

"So what's the plan?" Emily asked. "We just hop in the Jeep and drive to get help?"

I shook my head. "No. They made sure that we weren't leaving that way."

Sara froze. "What do you mean?"

"They slashed the tires and ruined the engine. That Jeep isn't going anywhere." When Sara's face fell, I quickly added, "But Officer Donnelly here has a truck that we can take. How far away did you park?"

"About a mile southeast of here."

"You think they could have gotten to it?"

He shook his head. "I parked where they couldn't find it. And it's so far away, the engine wouldn't alert them to my presence."

I frowned. "The flashlight would have alerted them." Then again, he didn't turn it on until I was nearly on top of him.

"I'm not lying." He groaned. "I figured if it all went to hell, I could pretend that I was here on official park business. Besides, I got to see things in the dark I wouldn't have otherwise." He smirked at that last part.

I just about died from embarrassment.

"We can also radio for help from the truck," he added, as if sensing that his comment nearly had me retreating into my shell.

I sucked in a deep breath. "Good, I like this plan."

"And call me Colton."

I wasn't sure if I could start calling him "Colton" without getting too close. You start calling a hot man by his first name, and then what's next? Ziplining through the Chattahoochee National Forest?

If I got back to Jacksonville yesterday, that wouldn't be

soon enough to get out of this mess.

"There's just one problem with that part," Sara said. "Who are we going to call for help? Animal control? We have *werewolves* that are hunting us. You don't just call the police on them."

I had to refrain from telling her that the werewolves were only hunting her. I figured that wouldn't go over very well.

"There's a local pack," he said. He got to his feet. "I'm a member. They'll take us in."

"And save us?" Emily asked, her voice trembling. "Because all I wanted was a vacation. I'd really like to be saved, please."

"Me too," I told her gently. "Just think how relaxed you'll be when you get home."

She shook her head. "I never thought Atlanta would seem safer than this."

"Join the club. Okay." I looked at Emily's pumps. "You aren't going to run in those, are you?"

Both Sara and Emily looked at me blankly. Only Officer Donnelly—*Colton*—knew what I had in mind and he nodded in understanding.

"What?" Emily asked.

"We're going to make a run for the car. You can't do that in high heels, hun."

She blanched. "All of us? But you two are the monsters—werewolves—*magic people*," she finally managed. "Why don't you go out to grab the truck and bring it back here?"

"That's what I thought you were proposing, too," Sara added.

"There's at least six wolves out there," Colton said. "Seven, if you count your friend. I could smell them on my way to the cabin. If Christine and I go get the truck, we can come back quickly, but that's leaving you two in danger. And if one of us goes, that's still splitting us up and they'll pick us off one by one. So the best thing to do is to go together."

"We can protect each other better then," I said. "Unless you have a better idea."

Emily was silent for a moment. "I don't have anything else to wear."

I pulled out my hiking boots from my bag. "I may pack light," I said pointedly to Sara, "but I do pack the essentials. Wear these."

***

Colton took point while I carried the rear. I've never been in a true combat situation, except for my jiu jitsu classes that I took for self-defense, but we just naturally fell into formation like that. Sara and Emily were in the middle, the safest place for humans.

I hoped I didn't look as terrified as them. Emily's eyes looked like they were about to bulge out and Sara kept jerking her head around at any slight movement.

Trust me, if it was dangerous, I'd know even before we heard the noise.

When we got to the main level of the cabin, I inwardly groaned as it was raining outside. Lucky bastards. I won't be able to smell them as easily.

Colton's eyes met mine and he gave the barest nod. He was thinking the exact same thing. Sure, the rain masked them, but it also gave us an advantage too. We just had to make sure that we could follow through with it.

"Calm down, Sara," I muttered to my sister. "I can hear your heartbeat racing at a million miles a minute."

Emily looked at me, shocked. "You aren't going to drink her blood, are you?"

I inwardly groaned. "I'm a werecat, not a vampire." At her blank look, I added, "I don't drink blood. It's just bad because I can hear her from across the room. I think once we get outside, the rain will cover it up, but we all need to calm down."

Sara gulped and nodded. "Sorry," she whispered. "I'm just so scared."

"I am too," I said gently. "But we'll get out of this. Okay, now we need to be quiet."

We reached the front door. I kept an ear open as I looked out behind us. Colton propped the door open a slight bit, stuck his head out, and then signaled for us to follow.

Outside, the rain was even worse, coming down in buckets. Immediately, I was soaked to the bone, making me wish that I had transformed. Mountain lion fur is amazingly waterproofed compared to cotton and human skin.

In the distance, I heard thunder rumble. The rain on the already-wet ground and on the leaves covered up a lot of noises, and all I could smell was the dampness in the air.

The only way they could find us was by sight, and it was hard through the rain and trees. I hoped.

Please, please, please let us get there in one piece.

We moved as a pack to a copse of trees about a hundred feet from the cabin. The significance of the word "pack" wasn't lost on me. Werecats had a social order, but nothing like werewolves. They lived and died by the pack, and to lose a potential member like Sara would have been a huge blow to their morale.

Ugh, shifter politics.

I could only hope that Sara wouldn't have to experience it like I did. Emily too, for that matter. I didn't know what the wolves would do if they got their claws on her, but I didn't like the thought of it. Many people join the were community against their will. Including me. And many of them don't last.

They weren't as lucky as me.

With the rain, thunder, and darkness, we were practically running blind. Even with my cat-like eyes, I had trouble having a good grasp on what was happening around us. A mile seemed like a long way in these conditions, even to myself.

Thank god we had the good officer with us.

We followed Colton as he directed us further into the woods. I may have been a mountain lion shifter, but I was a city girl at heart, so running around in the woods at night was out of my comfort zone. I was grateful for the fact that he was here.

Not just because he's good-looking.

Certainly not that at all.

If I wasn't much for the outdoors, Emily was in her exact opposite environment. She slipped and fell in the mud several times trying to keep up with us. I saw her tear-stained face every time lightning struck. Sara wasn't much better. But she at least had the air of someone who knew where to place her feet; Emily was woefully lost.

We paused underneath a rock outcropping to catch our collective breath. Or rather, Emily's and Sara's breaths.

"How much further?" Sara asked.

"Not too much farther," Colton told her. "Maybe another quarter mile or so."

"I want a bubble bath when all this is done," Emily sighed, putting a hand to her face. "I *deserve* a bubble bath."

And she started to cry. Sara comforted her, but I could tell that Emily was angry with her because she shrugged off the offered hug. Granted, I didn't blame her for being prickly to Sara.

"Do you think they're following us?" I muttered to Colton, so low that they couldn't hear.

"I've been trying to keep an ear out," he said softly, "and I haven't heard anything."

"Neither have I," I whispered back.

But we both knew that didn't mean anything.

"You never did tell me why we could trust you," I said, a note of playfulness in my voice. *Oh my god, am I flirting?* The thought struck me like a ton of bricks. No, I was just trying to make this terrible situation better for all of us. I was scared out of my mind, and there were lives on the line. That was what they called comic relief, right?

Colton smiled—and I began to think of all his smiles as being wolfish.

"Because I'm the best hope you've got," was his answer. Not the greatest response, but I thought he was flirting back, judging by the way he was smiling.

"I can handle myself too, you know," I said.

"Yeah," he said honestly. "You can. How did you get caught up in this anyway, if you don't mind me asking?"

"Sara's my sister." That usually explained a lot of things.

But Colton shook his head. "No, I mean caught up as a were. When did that happen?"

I snorted through my nose. "It was bad decision that I made a long time ago for the guy I loved."

The sparkle in his blue eyes lost their luster. "So there's a Mr. Were Mountain Lion?"

I combed a hand through my sopping wet hair. "There was. Not anymore."

And that was all I was going to say on that subject.

Colton nodded, catching the fact that I clammed up when it came to my past and my relationship with Shane.

We didn't have time to deal with the past anyways, so I pushed it towards the back of my mind.

We were in a life and death situation. There was no time for any of that.

"We'd better keep a move on," I announced, my voice slightly strangled. It was sometime after two or three a.m., and I wanted to get as far away from here as possible by sunrise.

Everything was less scary in the daytime. But you also can't hide as easily.

CHAPTER 11

I DIDN'T REALIZE HOW MUCH I'D DOUBTED that Colton's truck would be in working order until we actually came upon it—and it was fine. None of the tires were slashed, the hood wasn't dented. It was in the exact same condition it had been in earlier today, albeit much wetter and muddier.

I sighed a breath of relief as I saw it. Actually, it was more like a sob—relief straddled that line pretty easily.

Colton hadn't been lying when he said that the truck was well-hidden. It was off the dirt road a ways and shielded by the trees around it. I wouldn't have seen it unless I was looking for it.

Hopefully our attackers weren't looking for it as well.

Colton took his keys out, and unlocked the car. I winced as the lights flickered on and off, afraid that it would tell the werewolves that we now had transportation. But I didn't have time to dwell on that as we piled into the car.

As I helped Sara into the back seat, Colton leaned into the truck, grabbed the handset for the CB radio, and called for help. "Officer Donnelly, Dispatch." He took his finger off and looked at me. I held my breath, waiting for an answer.

Nothing. The silence from the radio was long enough for my brain to freak out.

"Is the radio broken?" I asked.

Colton shook his head. "No. There's nothing wrong with the radio." I opened my mouth to say otherwise, but he turned away from me. "Officer Donnelly, Dispatch. Respond, dammit."

Finally, there came, "Dispatch, Officer Donnelly. Dispatch, Officer Donnelly!" The man on the other end sounded flustered, like we had just caught him on the john.

Colton gave me an I-told-you-so smirk and responded, breaking all protocol for police radio conversations that I've seen on TV. I had the feeling that they didn't follow the rules to the letter here. Which was fine with me, so long as we got going. He checked his GPS monitors. "Vicks, my location is at 34.823178, -83.563758. Are there any other rangers in the area?"

"Lemme have a look," Vicks said on the other end.

I glanced behind us, out into the darkness. I couldn't help but feel like we were being watched. We were sitting ducks out here, wasting time talking on the radio. It felt like it took all too long for Vicks to come back onto the line.

"The closest to your location is Barnett. And he's thirty minutes away."

Donnelly cursed under his breath. He met my eyes, and I nodded. I knew exactly what that meant.

We were on our own.

"Copy that," Donnelly said. "We're headed your way."

"We?"

"Some ladies who have been assaulted," Donnelly said. "I'll get back to you when we're close."

"Copy that."

"Over and out."

Colton hung up the mouthpiece and combed a hand through his hair, obviously distressed that help was so far away.

Whose idea was it to go camping in such a remote area? Oh yeah, my sister's.

"What's happening?" Emily asked, her voice bordering on shrieking.

"Nothing," I said. "We just need to get going." *And figure this out when we're in a safer place.*

Just before I hopped into the passenger seat, Colton pressed the keys into my hand.

"Wait, what are you doing?" I asked.

"I'm going into the bed of the truck," he explained. As if I should have guessed that. "That way if they ambush us, I'm ready to fight."

I agreed with him to an extent. Transforming in closed quarters like the cab of a truck was never a good idea. "I don't know where I'm going."

He pointed down the road. "You just take that road and don't stop 'til you hit the highway."

I was pretty sure that it was more complicated than that, but I nodded. As long as it was away from the cabin, that was all I cared about.

I gulped. "All right then. I can do that."

I pulled myself up into the driver seat and chuckled at myself. If anything, being in the driver's seat only reinforced how much bigger Colton was than me. I readjusted it, checked the mirror just in time to see Colton easily hop into the bed of the truck.

I swallowed back the lump in my throat.

"Everyone situated?" I asked. I didn't even wait for Emily's or Sara's response—I threw the truck into drive and hit the dirt road, mud and water sloshing all over the place.

I drove the unfamiliar truck, fighting the twisting, turning roads. There's nothing more terrifying than driving at a high speed through the woods in the middle of the night during a thunderstorm. Emily kept shrieking, making me want to crawl out of my skin. We had to remain calm. We had to get out of here.

My reflexes saw it before my eyes did; I slammed on the brakes, the truck skidding to a halt. Emily screamed, and I only narrowly avoided flipping the truck over.

A massive tree, that looked like it had been knocked out by lightning, blocked our way.

We all knew better.

And on top of that tree was a werewolf, its red eyes glowing their way towards us. Lightning struck, illuminated the beast, and I recognized it as the big one from my fight in the cabin's great room.

"Chad," Sara whispered, her eyes locked on the windshield.

So this was the bastard that terrorized my sister. I clenched the steering wheel, feeling my anger rise. There was no way he was going to get away with this. I was going to kill if I must in order to save Sara.

As if sensing my thoughts, the beast's orbs narrowed slightly. Another one joined him up on the log, and I recognized her instantly from her smell.

Andrea.

"Colton!" I screamed, my voice raising in pitch. I refused to look behind me to see if he was still there. I didn't want to take my eyes off the monster in front of us.

I didn't have a choice in the end. The doors to the cab tore off in a shower of metal and bolts, revealing snarling snouts. The monsters grabbed at me, at Sara, and at Emily, forcibly pulling us from our restraints. Seatbelts broke, glass shattered, chaos broke out.

"Sara!" I shrieked. "Emily!" I reached for them, but the monsters were too fast. They were out of my grasp before I could do anything to stop it.

A roar joined my shriek, and it took me a moment to realize that Colton had joined the charge. I closed my eyes, calling forth the beast in my mind.

Time to become the mountain lion.

I roared, surprising my assailants, who abruptly let go of me. I fell to my paws on the ground, and lunged at them, catching one of them in the face. They were stunned at my attack; moving slower than expected.

Apparently, they hadn't known which one of us could shift into a mountain lion. I used that to my advantage.

As I moved away from the truck, I found that my friends were being dragged away, their terrified expressions pleading with me to save them in any way I could.

A large body landed next to me, and I cast one glance to make sure that it was Colton. I bared my teeth at him, telling him to pursue them alongside me. He bristled in response, a huge, hulking beast, and I made a mental note not to get on his bad side.

I seriously wished we could communicate to each other. We'd have to go off body language, which lost a bit in translation.

We charged, running towards the beasts. We almost got there, except something attacked me on my right-hand side, crunching ribs and tearing fur as I sprawled to the ground. I growled and looked up into blood-red eyes.

Chad.

I froze as he snarled down at me. Spittle dripped down onto my face and I winced, not wanting that vile liquid to land on me.

He had me pinned, and we both knew it. He could tear out my throat here and now, and end it. It was amazing in that moment, because a sense of hopeless peace descended upon me.

This is where it ends.

A roar sounded and Chad was thrown off me. I rolled

to my side, enough to see Colton and Chad brawling. I only realized now how evenly matched they were. Both big beasts, both skilled at fighting. A strange thought crossed my mind:

Colton's an alpha?

I didn't have long to ponder that, because teeth grabbed me by the scruff of my neck. Not just one set of them; a few. How many wolves were here, I would never know, but it seemed like they all ganged up on me and pulled me away. I recognized one as Andrea. The others were unfamiliar, but it panged my heart that our so-called friend continued to betray us.

I dug into the ground with my claws, screaming, although I didn't know who could have helped me at that moment. Sara and Emily were being kidnapped, Colton was in a fight, and I was being literally dragged away. My claws tore on the dirt, catching rocks and debris. I started bleeding, both from the teeth in my neck and from my futile efforts to stay put.

"Christine!" Sara screamed, so far away.

I looked up, and our eyes connected. She was pleading with me to fight.

Except it was no longer my choice. With one heave from my assailants, my claws left the ground and I flew out into empty space. Darkness swallowed me as I fell, the roar of water below rushing up to greet me.

I heard a howl of—anguish?—before I hit the unyielding river, swollen from the rain. I didn't have time to fight the waves as my head struck a rock.

And I remembered nothing more.

CHAPTER 12

THE SMELL OF COFFEE WOKE ME UP.

Man, that was a great idea. Because as I swam out of sleep, I realized how much caffeine I'd need to function this morning. I'd have to thank Sara or Emily, because with this splitting headache, I don't think—

I froze, taking stock of my situation before I opened my eyes. My head was killing me, and I gingerly felt for the knot on my skull. My fingers met bandages, and a quick inspection told me that it wrapped around my entire head.

I opened my eyes—or rather, my left one, because I still couldn't open my right eye—grimacing in the bright sunlight. I was on the couch in some sort of sunroom. A quick glance outside confirmed that I was still somewhere out in the woods, although where exactly, I wasn't sure.

"Ugh." My entire body ached. I had bandages and ice packs all over my body. I'm sure I looked like a boxer who just lost a match.

"Morning sleepyhead," a voice greeted me.

I blinked, not recognizing it. It was an elderly woman's voice, and that didn't fit any of the people I last remembered talking to. I turned my head to see a woman, somewhere in her eighties, peering down at me over her horn-rimmed glasses. She looked spritely, like she could tackle me even now, and not just because I was so injured.

"Good…morning?" I asked, utterly confused.

She grinned. "Coffee's almost done. And I'm sure you have a ton of questions."

"Yes. I do."

She put a hand on my shoulder. "The most important thing is, you're safe for now."

I frowned. "And my friends?"

Her expression darkened. "That's something my grandson needs to talk to you about."

"Grandson?" I pushed myself up to a sitting position, even though every muscle and organ protested doing so.

"Hey."

I recognized this voice. And I quickly made sure that I was covered, because the last time I remembered being conscious, I was a mountain lion shifter, which meant that clothes never stayed intact.

Happily, I was in a frilly nightshirt, probably courtesy of the lady here. Who I just realized was Colton's grandmother.

"You're at my place," Colton explained. Gauze covered his right ear, which confirmed that he was in just as bad a shape everywhere else as me. "You fell into the river and I saved you."

The old lady beamed, like she was the proudest grandma in the world.

"And Sara and Emily?" I asked, narrowing my eyes.

He hesitated. "They were taken."

"And you couldn't stop them?"

He shot me a cool look. "I had a decision to make, and I saved you. They'll be all right, at least for now. You, on the other hand, would've drowned."

My stomach roiled. I must have looked sick because the grandma handed me a waste basket. I emptied the contents of my stomach into it, which admittedly wasn't a lot.

Sara.

Emily.

Lost to those werewolves.

I failed them. They were my responsibility and I let them down.

"It's going to be all right, Sugah," the grandma said. I highly doubted that, but I didn't say anything as she took the waste basket from me, and rose to her feet to dispose of it, leaving Colton and me alone.

"I did what I thought was best," he said sheepishly, as if that answered everything. Sheepish from a wolf; Colton seemed to be at odds with himself.

I put my aching head in my hands, allowing myself to sob for a moment. I couldn't believe that this was happening. I needed time to think, to figure things out. To save them.

"Do you think that Sara is a fully-fledged werewolf now?" I asked, my voice raspy.

He averted his eyes. "I don't know," he answered

truthfully.

My hopes sank further, and I gulped down some air. It didn't seem like I was getting enough oxygen.

"I will say this, though," he said gently. "The sun rose only an hour after I fished you out of the lake."

"What does that mean?" I didn't mean to sound as harsh as I did.

"It means," he said pedantically, "that I don't think they would have forced your friend to become a werewolf; there wasn't enough time."

"How so?"

He snickered. "We kind of like theatrics with our rituals. At least that's how it works in my pack."

I almost snorted out loud. Werewolves and theatrics? The group of mountain lions that I interacted with when I was married to Shane had no room for things like that. They were just the rough and ready kind of folk who wanted things done quick and dirty. If werewolves wanted things done right, that was yet another difference between our species.

But that gave me hope.

"So we have until the next full moon for them to try again?"

His hard expression dashed my hopes on the ground. "The moon is full for three nights," he said. "It's not, technically, but it's enough for us to make that first transformation."

"So that means..."

He nodded. "They'll do it tonight if we don't stop them."

That jolt of awareness brought me to my feet. I groaned, swaying slightly as my stomach threatened to unload again. I hit my head pretty hard, apparently.

"You're not going to help anyone in that condition," Colton said.

"I have to do something!" I twisted away from him, stumbling as the pain hit me. "Ow…"

"This should help her." His grandma's voice brought both of our attention to her in the door. She held a steaming mug of coffee, which she pressed into my hands. "Drink."

I took a big sip, and the taste of whiskey filled my senses. I nearly spit the entire thing out. Instead, I managed to swallow it past the lump in my throat, but it burned all the way down.

"Grandma," Colton groaned.

"I put a shot of whiskey in there to help you wake up," she said, almost proudly.

I coughed. "I can tell."

True to his grandma's word though, I could feel it immediately helping. The mix of caffeine and alcohol both heightened my senses and dulled the pain. I took another sip, and now that I was prepared, it actually tasted good.

I took another sip.

"Does she know?" I asked, nodding to his grandma with my head. Being a shifter isn't inherited, at least not biologically. I knew a lot of people who "keep it in the family", but I wanted to make sure that his grandma was in the know.

"Call me Siouxsie," she said.

I liked her.

"Yes, she knows that I'm a werewolf." It was actually adorable seeing him blush about his grandmother's spunk. "She was the leader of the pack before me."

So he is an alpha. My suspicions from last night were correct.

"A long time ago, I told Colton not to get caught up in this stuff," Siouxsie sighed. "But he's as hardheaded as he is handsome. He asked when he was eighteen and his grandfather turned him. Remember that, Colton?"

He combed a hand through his hair, wincing at the movement. "Yes, of course."

I almost expected Siouxsie to pinch his cheeks or something, so I averted my eyes before I could burst out laughing. At least I could still laugh right now.

"Okay, so I can ask you point blank then," I said, leaning against the couch. "This ritual…what goes into it?"

He crossed his arms and focused his full attention on me as if he could completely shut out his grandmother's wry look. "In order to be turned into a werewolf, you first have to be bitten by one. As a failsafe, because we can get a little…rowdy at times…in order for someone to become a full-fledged werewolf, they have to have their first blood."

"What does that mean?"

He sighed. "It means that the sire first draws blood on

a human victim. And then the werewolf-to-be drinks it."

I made a face. "Like a vampire?" And that confirmed for me that Emily was the one who was most at risk. Because these wolves had kidnapped her, and I could imagine that she was the easiest to access.

"Except we're talking about werewolves," Siouxsie corrected.

Yet still, Emily's question about drinking blood earlier was oddly accurate. I made a mental note about that. "So then they can turn into a werewolf?"

Siouxsie nodded. "Why, how does your kind do it?"

"For mountain lion shifters, it's less…rigid." I shrugged, being swept up in memories. "Your sponsor starts licking you, cleaning you. Then others join in. And then it just ends up becoming a cleaning marathon."

Colton had a look of disgust, which made me smile lightly. At least we could still have a sense of humor with all of this stuff.

"Do you have any idea where they would perform that sort of ritual?" I asked.

He shrugged. "After last night, I doubt they'd do it here."

"Why?"

He actually looked offended at my question. "I have my pack on the lookout for them, and I put out an APB. If they pop up anywhere in a hundred-mile radius, we'll find them."

"Even in the woods like this?"

"We're wolves, Christine," Siouxsie said. "We'll know if there's anyone in our territory."

"Like you did last night?"

He bristled. "There's no law against wolves traveling through our territory. We're not savages. I knew that Andrea was a werewolf, but she's a part of the Atlanta pack. She's allowed to vacation here."

I guess that's what she meant by her life was in Atlanta. She said that her brother renovated the cabin five years ago. Was her brother a werewolf too?

Colton continued, oblivious to the fact that my mind was running a thousand miles a minute. "I had no idea that your friend was running away from them when I saw you at the gas station. Or that Andrea was in on it."

"Neither did I," I said icily, "but the end result is the same."

"I'm trying to find them."

"*We* need to go out and find them. Call for help, *whatever*," I said, exasperated. "And why are you smiling?"

He was. And it was irritating me. Why was he smiling so coyly when I was so distraught over my friends' kidnapping?

"Because you're pretty when you're flustered. Nothing more." He sighed before getting up. "It's about ten in the morning right now, so you should probably get ready. We'll head into Atlanta."

"Why Atlanta?" I asked.

Both grandmother and grandson looked at me.

"Because if I know wolves," Siouxsie said, "and I've been one for sixty years now, they'll want to do it on their own home turf."

So we were trading the wilderness for the concrete jungle of Atlanta. And I had no idea how we'd find them in a city that massive.

CHAPTER 13

"YOU IN THERE, SUGAH?"

I stuck my head out from the shower, using the curtain to cover up my body. "Miss Siouxsie?" I called out blindly.

A plush towel was pressed into my hands. "Here," she said. "I think Colton's ready to go."

Of course he is.

As Colton's truck was somewhere out in the Georgia wilderness, we had to take another option for travel, which was apparently Siouxsie's old Jeep. Colton said that he had to check the oil and a few other things, which didn't inspire confidence in the vehicle. We were going to hit the road hard.

I used that time to take a quick shower. Something about the fur and claws always made me feel like I couldn't get clean. I felt like I was violated from my fight with the wolves. I scrubbed for as long as I dared.

But I still couldn't get completely clean, and I still felt like I'd been hit by a freight train.

"Clothes are laid out for you," Siouxie said. The steam cleared enough for me to see her face and the old woman winked at me. "You're a bit bigger than me, but I found some things that should fit. And a few changes for later."

Right, I didn't have any other clothes than the flowy nightgown I woke up in.

"Thanks," I said.

I rinsed off as fast as I could and when I stepped out from the shower a few minutes later, I saw that there was a t-shirt and a pair of mom jeans folded on the counter for me. Not bad. Not that I was being picky anyways. Although the shirt did say, "World's Number One Grandma". I bet Colton gave it to her when he was younger.

Siouxsie was in the living room when I emerged, reading a book on her Kindle. With a sinking feeling, I realized that I'd left my books back at the cabin. So much happened in such a short amount of time.

She set down her Kindle and her face crinkled into a wide grin as she looked up at me.

"He's out in the driveway, dearie." She got up from her seat and hugged me. "Take care of him."

"Me take care of him?" I asked, not sure if she realized that this was her grandson she was talking about. The big man that was a park ranger and an alpha werewolf. I was a fish out of water when it came to this stuff.

But Siouxsie just continued grinning at me. "He likes you, you know."

Oh. "I…"

She chuckled. "I know, he's silly. But Colton always fell hard for pretty girls. Especially when they're strong, independent women like you."

I hadn't dated much since I divorced Shane. Why would I, when I had such a bad experience? I'd rather be alone than risk that again. But, thinking about it, was Shane still controlling my life even though I hadn't seen him in a decade?

Still, I was tongue-tied. "I…"

"Oh, don't take it like a marriage proposal. Attraction is pretty instantaneous. Or has it been that long since you dated and you forgot?" It actually had been, and I pressed my lips into a fine line. She waved me away though. "I'm just stating the obvious. The big lug won't."

"Okay."

"Here's a few changes of clothes for you and Colton," Siouxsie said, handing me a tote bag with folded clothes and I also noticed a Tupperware bin full of cookies. "Lord knows you'll shred your clothes from shifting. Just don't do it more than three times, and you'll be fine. There's also a Febreze bottle in there. Because, well, you know. You don't want them being able to sniff you out." She sighed, crossing her arms, looking a little sad. "And, with that, you should get going." She nodded towards the door. "He's waiting."

"You're not coming?" Suddenly, I wanted a buffer between us. Not just because he was attracted to me, but because I was afraid that I was going to end up being attracted to him. And make bad decisions.

But Siouxsie shook her head. "These old bones of mine would just slow you down. I will be here when it's all over."

I hugged her. "Thank you so much," I whispered honestly. "For everything."

She hugged me back. "Don't mention it. Now go."

As I pulled away, her eyes caught me off guard. They sparkled in very much the same way that Colton's did and I fought a blush as we walked out to the driveway. Whatever it was with werewolves and their sparkly eyes, I'll never know.

For raining so much the night before, the morning was fresh and bright. Humidity made the shirt immediately stick to my body, but I marveled at how beautiful the area around me was. I saw the appeal of living out in the wilderness.

And there was the Jeep. An Army-green color, it was old and looked like it had been in a few wars. I wasn't even sure that it would be able to make it to the main road. There was no top, and the hood was up as a shirtless Colton bent over the engine. Hot damn, he was good looking without a shirt on. It was the first time I'd seen him shirtless in daylight, and I wouldn't mind seeing him like this more often.

The good thing about shifters was that we tended to lose our shirts all the time.

As if sensing my eyes on him, Colton stood to his full height and shut the hood. He gave me a grin, and I averted my eyes, remembering what Siouxsie said.

"Hey," he said. "Jeep's ready."

He took a towel and mopped the sweat off his body before putting on a tee that stretched a little too tightly across his biceps. That was almost as bad as him being shirtless.

"We're driving in that?" I asked, not meaning to sound off-putting.

"Yeah," he said. "It looks worse for wear, but it's built like a tank."

I knew that time was running out and there was no other option for us getting to Atlanta. It was either this or I was going to let Sara and Emily down. And I wasn't about to do that.

I took a deep, steadying breath. "Let's go."

***

SIOUXSIE'S WORDS DISTRACTED ME THE entire drive. Being stuck in a Jeep with Colton felt incredibly awkward after she told me that he was attracted to me. And then I found myself looking too long at Colton's biceps or wondering if those words were true. He kept it casual, watching the road, driving effortlessly when I had so much trouble in the rain the night before. He knew these back roads better than I knew swimming.

And I was a professional mermaid, so that said a lot.

He noticed my eyes on him at one point and shifted uncomfortably under my gaze. "What?"

"So you're the pack alpha?" I asked. Best to cover up

my staring with a blatant question.

He quirked an eyebrow, but answered. "Yeah."

"So what does that mean, exactly?"

He shrugged. "It's really just a title."

"I thought titles and rank were important in werewolf packs."

"Yeah. A bit." He frowned. "Okay, maybe a lot."

We drove in silence for a while before he sighed and acquiesced to my question. "It means that I'm the biggest wolf in the pack." I snorted, but he kept talking. "We help each other, while I protect them if something happens. We live and die by each other, and once a pack member, always a pack member. Yet, at any time, I can essentially pull rank on any of the lower wolves to do something that I want them to do. If my pack was a town, I'd be the mayor."

"So…to become the mayor of Werewolf Town," I said, using his metaphor, "are you voted in?"

He glanced at me. "What, mountain lions don't have alphas?"

"We more tolerate each other than anything else."

Thank god for that, too. I couldn't imagine being a werewolf in the same situation with Shane and getting out of that way of life with my hide intact. I managed to keep my job with Neptune's Mermaids, while Shane had to adhere to a restraining order. It also helped that I shamed him in front of the other werecats. Ruined my reputation, but it ruined his as well.

Colton's jaw moved slightly as he considered my

question. "You fight your way to the top. Not to the death or anything—except in *some* cases…" His voice trailed off, and I didn't press the question. "But that's extreme cases. And that didn't happen when I fought my way to alpha. Although I did end up—" he coughed "—fighting my grandma." He scratched his head. "I think she let me win."

"Why'd you do it?" I asked.

He smirked. "You ask a lot of questions, don't you?"

"I just want to know what we're up against." *And what kind of world Sara will be joining if we don't find her in time.*

He seemed to understand my meaning, and he nodded. "My grandmother talked about it, briefly. My family has been werewolves for the past seven generations up in this area."

I hummed the dueling banjos song and he laughed.

"Yes, exactly like that. But, we'd all been werewolves. And when I was eighteen, my older brother…" He stopped, and I realized that he was venturing into too-personal territory.

"You don't have to talk about that, if you don't want to," I said gently. I put my hand over his and gave a gentle squeeze, which, I realized after the fact, wasn't like me at all. But conversations between us were natural, and I wanted to comfort him like this.

Even though we just met. After last night and today, comfort was all we had left.

Colton let out a sigh and shook his head. "No," he said, his voice slightly strangled. "I should talk about it. My older brother, Stephen, was a werewolf, meant to carry on the family line. I was supposed to go out west somewhere like San Francisco and go to college. I wanted to be an English professor." He chuckled darkly, then sobered. "But then Paul got into a car wreck."

"I'm so sorry."

"It's been *years*, but we were close. So…I became a wolf to carry on the family line. Because it was expected, no matter what Grandma says." He gestured vaguely, and I got the idea that he was just trying to do something with his hands—anything to take his hand away from mine. Which was all right. "I had to carry on the family business. And I had to move up in the ranks." That wolfish smile was back, although it was bittersweet. "Being a lower wolf sucks, especially if you have a bastard of an alpha. Not that Grandma was a bastard."

"But Sara would be dealing with one," I said.

He nodded. "And she'd be stuck with them."

My stomach dropped at the thought. I couldn't bear the thought of her going through this. Based on what Colton said, her situation would be worse, and I wouldn't wish that upon anyone. Well, except maybe Shane and Andrea, the "friend" who betrayed us. Was she doing that of her own free will? Or did some alpha tell her to keep an eye on us?

How long have they been trying to turn Sara into a wolf?

So many thoughts were swirling in my head, I jumped when static crackled over Colton's handheld radio.

"Dispatch, Donnelly. Dispatch, Donnelly."

"Donnelly, copy," Colton said, holding the handset to his mouth. "Vicks is a werewolf too," he added so that only I could hear. "My right-hand guy, really. I'm having him keep an eye out for suspicious activity."

After the initial, proper greeting, Vicks went into casual conversation with Colton. "Do you remember Connie Sue at the Gas 'n Pass?"

Gas 'n Pass? Why did that sound familiar?

"Yeah," Colton said into the handset.

"Well." Vicks hesitated. "Godwin saw a bunch of wolves go in there early this morning. Connie Sue was on duty and didn't report anything."

Colton's face darkened. "Do you think she got the alert to look out for a bunch of wolves too late?" he asked.

"If so, why hasn't she reported it since?" Vicks asked.

"True. You've got a point." Colton accelerated the Jeep to go even faster and we began bouncing down the road at an even faster clip. I held onto the frame for dear life as we flew down the road. "Heading out her way. Will let you know what comes out of it. Good job, Vicks."

"Thanks." The other man sounded grateful for the compliment. It was direct evidence of the pack structure. "I'll keep an ear out for any more."

"Over and out," Colton said for good measure.

He put the handset down and looked at me. "We're going back to the gas station from yesterday," he said evenly. "And Connie Sue, the attendant that you met? She's a wolf herself."

I remembered the attendant that flirted with Colton. They seemed more familiar than just a park ranger and a gas attendant. They were in the same pack.

I froze remembering that Andrea ran in ahead of us. And it had been her suggestion to stop there, as it was "on the way". She must have run in there, alerted Connie Sue or called someone from the Atlanta pack before Emily, Sara, and I went in there.

"So if she didn't report a bunch of werewolves after receiving an alert," Colton said, gritting his teeth, "then we have a traitor on our hands."

"There are quite a few traitors in Werewolf-Town," I whispered. Colton glanced at me. "I think Andrea ratted us out even then. They were working together. They knew we were coming."

CHAPTER 14

"OFFICER DONNELLY," THE ATTENDANT hailed from the counter as we entered the convenience store. "Two days in a row. I should be honored. And you," she said, her gaze falling on me. "Welcome back!"

She seemed just as cheery as she did yesterday, which made my stomach twist into knots. Maybe this was all a big mistake. And maybe Colton and I were going to entering a trap by coming in here and threatening her.

But he proceeded anyways.

"Did you get my alert?" Colton asked. "About the persons of interest and kidnapping?"

Connie Sue nodded gravely. "Absolutely. Terrible situation, that."

Colton glanced at me, and I could read it in his eyes. *Lying.* I moved closer to the entrance of the store. I didn't know if there was a back entrance, but I wanted to make sure that she wasn't leaving through those barred doors.

"So why," Colton asked, turning his attention back to the attendant, "would Godwin have spotted a pack of seven werewolves—fitting my exact description—stop at this gas station, and I haven't heard anything from you?"

I saw the immediate change in Connie Sue. The cheeriness evaporated like water on a hot stove, replaced by unadulterated fear. She knew she was caught.

And she chose that moment to bolt.

Faster than I could follow, Colton reached out, grabbed her by the wrist and pulled her over the counter, snarling in her face. He had partially shifted; his hands were both long, with monstrous claws and his face was an anthropomorphic wolf's.

All the better to see you with, my dear.

"That was all the answer I needed," he said. "Connie Sue, you have betrayed our bloodlines, our faith, our trust—"

The woman screamed, something between a howl and shriek. It split my ears, making my headache worse. He held her fast, but she twisted away, shifting into her wolf self as she did so. Apparently, the entrance wasn't the only way out of there, because she scrambled along the floor, aiming for the area with the bathrooms.

I was expecting that.

I shifted into a mountain lion as I moved to intercept her. She came up short in front of me, and I saw the confusion on her wolf-face. She hadn't been expecting another were in her presence.

Too late for that now.

I growled at her, barring her path. The she-wolf howled unhappily and paced. As a human, Colton closed the gap between us, effectively closing her in. She was trapped, and we all knew it. Her eyes went wild and she acted like a caged animal, glaring at me with those unnerving eyes.

I knew that if I let off an inch, she'd go all over me. I tried looking as intimidating as possible in front of her. Maybe she was smart enough to get the hint. I doubted it though.

"Connie Sue, transform back into a human," Colton said tiredly. "Christine can't understand you when you're both different animals."

Connie Sue snapped at him once, but he stepped towards her threateningly and she cowered, her tail between her legs. A second later, she shifted back into a human, and quickly moved to the souvenir stand to put on a huge, oversized shirt that said, "Georgia on my mind."

The woman looked flustered, terrified out of her mind. I didn't blame her. But she started speaking, to my relief.

"Speak," Colton commanded. I *felt* the authority in his voice at that moment, and I realized why he was the alpha of his pack. He commanded the wolves with an iron fist when he needed to.

Connie Sue nodded, her eyes darting between him and me, as if debating who to speak to. "They contacted me about a week ago." Her voice was soft, almost ashamed. "They said that a wanted wolf-to-be was going to come through here with two other women and a fellow werewolf. They said that I was to alert them when that happened."

"Why'd you help them?" Colton asked, his voice low and dangerous.

She blanched. "I wanted to get away from here." Her eyes shot daggers at him. "I wanted to get out of this hell hole. And they offered me a place in their Atlanta pack. One where I'm not working at a gas station because some big guy tells me to."

"You were excited to take it," Colton said.

"Yeah, well, I hate it."

She must have been the world's greatest actress. I thought she liked her job from earlier. Her cheeriness, her smile...they felt genuine.

Colton's face went very neutral before he sighed and pinched the bridge of his nose, cursing under his breath. "You could have just asked, Connie Sue. There are no laws keeping you here."

"Except the pack," she shot back.

"And I make the laws of the pack."

She scoffed. "You wouldn't have let me leave."

"Don't tell me what I would and wouldn't have done," Colton growled.

She shrank back underneath his gaze, and if she wasn't partly responsible for Sara's and Emily's disappearance, I would have felt bad for her. As it was...I felt nothing towards her.

"You know that in other packs, treason is punishable by death." Colton kept his eyes on her as he spoke, using that power to intimidate her. "You're not getting off to a good start by betraying this one."

She shivered. "What are you going to do?"

He considered his answer, his eyes flicking to me for a response. I didn't know what to say, as this wasn't in my wheelhouse—not to mention that I was still in mountain lion form and he wouldn't be able to understand me. Even if he did, I didn't know what their pack rules were. If treason was punishable by death, I'd have been killed by my fellow werecats when I divorced Shane. I hurt him badly. But then again, he hurt me back.

Still though, she ratted Sara out. Sara, who had done nothing wrong. Sara, who meant well, even when she messed everything up.

But we needed to know where they were. That thought dampened the rising anger in my body.

Colton nodded, as if reading my thoughts. "Tell us where they went, and there'll be a lesser punishment." He quirked a smile. "Such as banishment to some place else."

It was far less than what she deserved. I couldn't believe that he'd just let her off like that, essentially giving her exactly what she wanted, but he knew our priorities. He knew that we had to get Sara and Emily back.

And I guess we'd never have to deal with her again. I could live with that.

Connie Sue looked at him, astonished, before closing her mouth, and then nodding quietly. "Atlanta, they're going to Atlanta."

At least we were traveling in the right direction. For some reason, even though Atlanta was its own concrete jungle, it seemed easier to navigate than the wilderness.

"Do you have any more than that?" Colton asked. "Do they have two women with them?"

Connie Sue licked her lips. "Yes."

"Any idea of where they're going in Atlanta, then?"

She shook her head. "No," she said, only halfway apologizing. "I have no idea. I didn't think to ask that, because I was happy that I was getting out of this hellhole."

That was no good. I moved behind the aisle, the same one where she grabbed a shirt, and called back my werecat, transforming me back into a human. I grab my own "Georgia on my mind" oversized t-shirt to put on temporarily.

"Can you find out?" I asked. "My sister has been kidnapped by one of them, and they're going to turn her into a full werewolf tonight. She doesn't want to join our world. And she's going to be in the same position as you in a few years, wanting to get out."

Connie Sue blinked at me, like she couldn't believe that I was the same woman who came through the gas station the day before.

"*Please*," I added for good measure, trying to appeal to her humanity, if there was any left.

She nodded to Colton. "So long as he promises that I'm free of any sort of treason charge."

Colton's upper lip curled, but I shushed him before he could say something to ruin all of it. "Yes, he promises. Just please see if you can find out."

She narrowed her eyes, waiting.

"Yes," Colton grunted, "fine. I promise not to punish you and you can go wherever the hell you want, so long as it's not here."

Despite his angry words, her face broke into a huge, wide grin, and I felt slightly sick that she was going to get her way. People like her didn't deserve a happy ending.

But I bit my tongue.

"Let me make a few phone calls," she said. "And see if anyone knows where the initiation is taking place tonight."

Did I trust her? No, but she was the only one who could help us right now.

She moved behind the counter, and pulled out her cell phone. Amazing how she was able to get reception out here when I couldn't, but then again, I was on a cheap prepaid plan, so it shouldn't surprise me that she had a better network. Still, I wondered how things could have changed if I only had reception.

"You okay?" Colton asked me, coming up to my right. His voice was low, to the point where it was breathy and it tickled my ear. It was to keep her from overhearing our conversation, but I still had to gulp down my nerves as he spoke to me like that.

I nodded. "I mean, I can't believe she'd do something like that, but then again, she seems desperate to get out of here." I looked up at him. "Would you have really killed her for betraying your pack?"

He hesitated before answering. "That's a question for later."

I didn't know if that meant he would or if he wouldn't. But I hugged my arms to my body and shivered nonetheless. His gaze softened at that.

"Let's just say I'm not a monster," he said, offended.

I frowned as he walked towards Connie Sue, who was busy on the phone, and I focused on her conversation again. From my vantage point, I could hear the person on the other end, but the quality of the call wasn't great.

That made me feel better about not having great reception.

"...Well of course I want to go, I'm going to be a part of the pack now, right?" Connie Sue said in the receiver, her voice that cheery attendant-speak from earlier. She really was a great actress—she should try Hollywood. She turned around and froze when she realized that Colton was coming closer to her. She gulped and nodded. "Yes, yes. Okay. I'll see you there. 8pm on the dot."

She hung up and addressed Colton, her voice slightly uneven.

"They're doing it at Old Plow Company, tonight at eight o'clock."

I frowned. "What's that?"

She shrugged. "Look, I don't know. I just know that they're taking her there. And that I'm betraying the Atlanta pack by doing this."

"It didn't seem to bother you to betray ours," Colton sneered.

Connie Sue widened her eyes. "Well, that's because…"

Colton waved her away. "I don't want to hear it. You have my word that I won't execute you, but you'd better be gone by the time I'm back here."

She froze. "When would that be?"

"As soon as possible."

It felt like he wasn't joking. And from the fear in Connie Sue's eyes, she believed him too.

"Let's go, Christine," Colton said, looking at me. "We've got another three hours at least to get there, and I want to be ready."

I think Connie Sue passed out from relief as soon as we left the gas station. And as I put on my second change of clothes in the backseat while Colton drove (not exactly legal, but hey, I was with law enforcement), I wondered how many times I'd have to change clothes trying to find Sara and Emily.

***

NOT TOO LONG AFTER WE LEFT THE GAS station, my phone beeped with text messages and emails galore. I frantically checked through them to see if there was anything from Sara, on the slim chance that she had access to a cell phone.

"Anything?" Colton asked, as he kept his eyes on the road.

I shook my head, unable to hide my disappointment. "No. Nothing."

"It'll be all right." His fingers drummed on the steering wheel. "We'll get there in time. We'll stop them. Your sister will be all right."

Would she? I hoped so.

We had alerted the rest of the wolves in Colton's pack that they were in Atlanta, although they couldn't exactly come down here without inciting a war. A few were coming down, although they'd arrive too late. Colton also radioed the Atlanta police, telling them to keep an eye out for two women fitting Sara's and Emily's descriptions.

But, for all intents and purposes, Colton and I were Sara's and Emily's only hope.

I saw that I had a text from Alaina, showing a picture of her newborn baby boy. She looked absolutely smitten at the new addition to her little family. Lucas, her son, was about three weeks old, and cuter than any baby I'd seen. And that's not just because I'm biased because it was a friend's baby.

He really was adorable.

The text was accompanied by a simple, "Hope all is well in your world."

I smiled despite myself and responded with a quick, "You too. <3."

I wasn't going to burden her with my worries. She wouldn't believe me, just like I didn't believe Sara when she approached me about her problems. Besides, I didn't want to drag her into this world—she obviously has enough to worry about with Lucas on her hands. She didn't even know that I had gone on vacation. We'd drifted apart since she left the mermaids to raise her child.

Still though, the text warmed me up inside. Everything would be well. I was going to make sure of it.

I put the phone away and looked out the window.

"That yours?" Colton asked, breaking into my thoughts.

It took me a moment to realize that he meant the baby. He must have seen the picture when I was responding.

I chuckled in answer. "No, just a friend of mine. She had her baby not too long ago. Miracle baby."

"Miracle, eh?" he asked.

"Yeah. She had a difficult pregnancy." Why was I telling him this? He probably didn't care, but he didn't say anything, as if he waited for me to keep talking. So I did. "But the baby is healthy and everything is all right now—just goes to show you not to give up hope."

He nodded and looked at me. "Yes. Don't give up hope."

CHAPTER 15

I LEARNED LATER THAT OLD PLOW COMPANY was in Atlanta's Midtown, straddling one of the major arteries into Downtown. While I didn't know much about the city, it felt oddly strange for a big, secret werewolf initiation to take place in such an urbanized area. Like a constant reminder that we were never too far from nature's wild ways.

I also learned, when we pulled up to the address, that it was a massive complex of old buildings in the middle of renovations. Finding where it would happen wasn't going to be an easy task.

Colton drove the Jeep around the block once and I stuck my head out of the window, trying to see if there was any hint of cars pulling in or a grouping of them parked somewhere. We couldn't exactly come up and knock on the door to find out which building it was in.

The sun hung heavily on the horizon, like it was threatening me with sunset. I mentally begged it to hold on for a little bit longer. If we didn't find them before nighttime, then we'd be too late. A quick glance at the clock said it was almost 7pm. An hour away from when it was supposed to happen. But I wasn't about to hang around waiting.

"I don't see anything," I said, feeling disappointed as I slipped back into my seat. I fought back the rising panic. They were here. They had to be.

"I'm going to have to park down the street anyways," Colton said. He flicked his eyes to me. "It's going to be fine, Christine."

I was about to puke, my nerves getting the best of me.

He parked on a street about a half mile away from Old Plow Company. I jumped out, antsy as all hell. I couldn't think about anything other than fighting them. I mentally paced inside the cage of my mind, ready to leap out and tear out the throat of anyone who came near me.

I had to find them.

"We'll find them," Colton promised again, echoing my thoughts.

"What if they aren't here?" I asked for what seemed like the hundredth time.

"They'll be here," he answered grimly. "Because they *have* to be here."

So that was our plan? Hope for the best, that Connie Sue wasn't playing us as fools?

All the questions didn't make me feel better, but I grabbed the tote out of the backseat and Colton raised an eyebrow.

"You're a bit of a prude, aren't you?" he asked.

"I spend about four hours a day in a mermaid tail and a

bikini in front of children." I put the bag over my shoulder. "I'm like the kindergarten teacher of the aquarium—I'm highly conscious of being naked, so I am bringing some clothes."

At his confused frown, I sighed. "I'll tell you later." I hadn't told him what I did for a living on the drive over, and now wasn't the time. I dug in the tote bag and produced the Febreze bottle. "Let me spray you."

He smirked. "I thought that was a male thing?"

"Shut up," I said, laughing even though I should be worrying about so many other things. At least he took my mind off this. I could live with that.

We both sprayed each other with the Febreze, which may not have been environmentally or health friendly, but at least we didn't smell like ourselves. It masked our scents enough for the werewolf pack to be noseblind to us.

It also hindered our own sense of smell, but we'd have to live with that.

We also couldn't exactly shift and head over there. We were still in a very heavily populated area, and people wouldn't be too keen on seeing a wolf and a mountain lion roaming Atlanta. I'd prefer not to draw attention to ourselves.

Colton and I hurried down the sidewalk, a block away from the entrance to Old Plow Company. Colton led the way, frowning as he tried looking over the fence that lined the property, his nose gently sniffing the air. I tried that too, but there were too many unfamiliar smells in the area, and the Febreze ruined any scent that I got. So I just kept an eye on the horizon, watching that sun dip ever lower and lower.

"We're out of time," I whispered.

"No," Colton said, almost desperate. "We're not too late."

He looked up at the fence in front of us, sniffed once, and then looked at me. I watched him, perplexed as to what he was thinking, when he up and jumped the fence. He didn't climb it; he simply crouched and then sprang, executing a backflip before landing on his feet.

"Are you trying to impress me?" I hissed, feeling the blush in my cheeks. Because it totally did impress me. I guess he had more athletic prowess than his huge bulk suggested.

He chuckled. "Are you coming or not?"

I looked at the fence and the barbed wire. I could make it, but not as a human.

"Yeah," I grumbled, not looking forward to transforming again. I was making a habit of it now. "But that means that I'm going to be a werecat for the rest of the night." Especially since we didn't have time for me to undress and redress.

I hefted the tote bag over the barbed wire, glad when Colton caught it easily. I paced once, transforming as I walked. When I fell on all fours, I picked up the pace, going once more counter clockwise before I launched myself, narrowly avoiding the razor sharp barbed wire before landing on the other side. The impact jarred my joints and my aches protested as a reminder of the night before.

At least I didn't embarrass myself.

Colton grinned at me lopsidedly. "A cat always lands on her feet."

I bared my teeth at him in response, which made him chuckle and shake his head.

As a werecat, I sniffed the air, hoping that my sense of smell was better in my animal state. Smells were stronger, more vivid. And I picked up the barest hint of...

Sara.

I growled softly, hoping that Colton knew what I meant, and started running towards the scent. He followed behind me, slower since he was on two legs. We moved in the shadows of the buildings, avoiding the incandescent lights from the windows as twilight descended upon us. Old Plow Company was a combination of both fully renovated loft-like offices and empty warehouses. It was both a trendy place to work and a place in the middle of its transition.

There.

I smelled Sara in the big building, furthest from the road. The doors were boarded up, and construction equipment scattered around the site along with different building materials. This must have been one of the buildings that was not very far in its renovations. Making it the perfect place for a werewolf initiation.

But, seriously, how stereotypical was this? It felt like

something out of a movie. It seemed like the most obvious place for this sort of thing.

I wasn't about to let my guard down though. I bristled, walking up closer to the building. It was nestled next to a hill, so climbing up the hill gave us the advantage of being able to look through one of the high windows.

Hopefully the shadows and the Febreze would conceal us.

At first, I didn't see much, just one guy in a motorcycle jacket in the middle of the room as he inspected the area, setting up a pair of black chairs. A buddy of his came into view and he told the other guy off, pointing towards the door.

Colton pulled himself up beside me and my ear twitched at his close proximity. The Febreze masked most of his scent, but being this close to me, he was almost intoxicating. I tried focusing on the task at hand, but it felt so nice having a big gentleman right next to me.

I could get used to being around Smokey Bear.

I blocked that very thought from my mind as I watched a pair of men drag a woman to the chairs in the middle of the warehouse. They had put a black bag on her head, effectively blindfolding her and making it harder for me to identify who it was. I was about 90% sure it was Emily based on the way she walked and the prevalence of her scent—but I also smelled Sara.

Where is she?

Then I saw the pack emerge, completing a semicircle

around the chairs. I glanced at the other windows, seeing that their circle filled up most of the warehouse. I guesstimated that there were about fifty. *Fifty werewolves!* There was no way I'd be able to fight them off to get to Sara and Emily.

But when I watched one of them pull off the sack, revealing a terrified Emily, I found that, yes I did have the drive to fight. Because no one should be as scared as she was at that moment. I still didn't know where Sara was, which scared me.

Movement in the corner caught my eye and I let out a small gasp. Andrea was among the wolves here. She looked smug and crossed her arms.

I was going to pay her back for what she did to Sara.

I felt, rather than saw, the sun set, twilight transforming into night quickly. Too quickly. With the sun gone, the moon seemed to shine even brighter, as if enhancing its purpose tonight. It threw the entire complex into a silvery glow. I blinked, trying to shake the glare from my eyes.

But the werewolves sensed it too, and unlike me, they reveled in the full moon's glow.

As a collective group of humans, they threw back their heads and began howling, a high-pitched shriek that set my teeth on edge. This was completely unlike a were mountain lion's initiation, which seemed like less of a cult-ring and more of an intimate gesture.

This was something unearthly.

Colton sucked in a deep breath and grabbed my fur,

like I was his lifeline to remaining human. I found myself wondering if he too felt the pull of the full moon. Was he going to start howling too?

The pack transformed as they howled, each at different speeds. Clothes shredded, teeth elongated, fur erupted along their skin. With this many wolves transforming all at once, I saw so many shapes and variations. The fur ranged from black to white, different patterns, different ways of wearing their skins. Some seemed more comfortable than others. But the thing that struck me the most was the difference in their sizes. Some were the size of household dogs while some looked like massive grey wolves.

There was a definite pecking order to the wolves, and I bet size had a lot to do with it. I hoped Andrea was the runt of the entire pack.

Emily was crying, and even though I could barely hear it over the howls, I watched her scream at the top of her lungs, shaking her head against the onslaught.

I'm going to save you.

My nose twitched. There was another wolf that I recognized here. I didn't know exactly who it belonged to, but this werewolf was present last night at the cabin and in the woods.

I held my breath as I saw a big wolf step into view. Emily froze, her gaze falling on the wolf. She shook her head, using her feet to propel herself backwards, away from the wolf, but one of them held the chair in place, forcing her to face this big wolf.

I guessed that was Chad, a guess that was later confirmed when he turned back our way, beckoning with his head to bring someone else into view.

Sara.

The members of the pack that held her fast were mostly human still, pushing her forward into place. She struggled, kicking and screaming as Emily started crying even harder.

Why couldn't any of the other wolves see that neither of them wanted this?

I realized what was happening: Emily was a sacrifice to make Sara transform for the first time. Sara's first kill. Chad just had to draw her blood, and as terrified as Emily was at the moment, Sara's predatory instincts would kick in and she'd transform completely to wolf.

I saw it all clearly. And we needed to do something *now*.

I turned to Colton, pleading at him with my eyes. We had to save them. I wasn't about to let either of them be sacrificed like this.

He nodded and before I knew what was happening, he rushed towards the window, transforming as he did so. He was a complete wolf as he hit the glass at full speed, the window shattering around him as he leapt through it, making a grand entrance.

I didn't have time to wait and see what happened. A split second after he landed in the throng of wolves, I charged through the window myself, nicking my shoulder on a shard of glass, but I landed on my feet, snarling and hissing.

My injury burned, but I'd live. Because I needed to stop this insanity right now.

We caught the wolves off guard, which was a blessing, because they all stared at us, open-mouthed, wolves and humans alike. I bet they didn't expect us to have been able to track them all the way from the mountains to here. They weren't ready for another Alpha werewolf and a huge mountain lion to land in their midst.

We used that to our advantage. Colton ran straight for Chad, tackling him from the side. The two wolves clashed in a flurry of fur, spittle, and yelps, bristling at each other.

I used that moment to step between Sara and Emily, but I didn't know how to proceed from there. Should I knock away the human wolves that held Sara?

The two of them answered for me; they transformed into wolves and attacked me. I could tell by their size and height that they weren't too high within the society of werewolves, which explained why they were no better than henchmen, but two against one was unfair, even for a big mountain lion like me.

Still though, I showed them that I couldn't be messed with. I felt the fur along the ridge of my back stand up straight as I faced them. I snarled, and in the moment of their flinch, I attacked.

I caught one to the face barreled into one, and he spun once, hitting the floor with a thud, grimacing in pain. The other grabbed me by the scruff on my neck and I shrieked in pain. Still though, I grabbed him with my own jaws, and, since I was bigger, I pulled him off me and into a wall.

His teeth left deep grooves in my neck, adding to the growing number of injuries that I already had. I couldn't focus on the pain, not now.

"Christine!" Sara screamed, but it was too late. The throng of werewolves, for lack of a better phrase, dog-piled on top of me, keeping me from attacking. Teeth and claws and bodies pressed me into the floor, and I couldn't breathe.

A bit unfair, but I'd decided that nothing in the werewolf world was fair. I only hoped that Colton was faring better than me, but my head was held immobile and I couldn't see behind me.

The noises sounded terrible, and even though Febreze mixed in the air, the coppery smell of blood filled my nostrils. I hoped that meant that Colton had succeeded, but I knew that he was probably overpowered.

Like me.

Chad stepped into my line of view. Unlike before, he had transformed back into a man. And, unlike me, he was completely unembarrassed by his nudity. I hadn't seen him as a human before, but I could now identify him by his scent—and I could see why Sara had once found him attractive. He was lean, but toned and tall. Scratches marred his muscular torso, and he had a dark, full beard that was trendy in a lumbersexual way, as well as tattoos wrapping his arms and around his chest.

The kind of bad boy that you'd find in a romance novel.

He huffed in anger, his dark eyes glaring at me.

"Look at what the cat dragged in," he murmured.

The other werewolves thought that was hysterical, and they all laughed, even if they were in wolf form. The sound, halfway between a howl and a jackal's laugh, set my teeth on edge.

It wasn't even a funny joke.

Another figure came into view, naked as well. *Andrea.* The woman crossed her arms and glared down at me. "Who would have thought that Sara would bring a were mountain lion on our little camping trip?"

Chad shrugged. "It's made things interesting."

Andrea glowered at him. "And ruined the cabin."

I saw it then, the resemblance in their red hair and facial structures. Chad was Andrea's brother, probably the brother who had renovated the cabin five years ago. This was all sorts of messed up.

It was like he planted Andrea to get to Sara.

"Sara, I have to hand it to your friend's tenacity," Chad said, drawing my attention back to him.

My sister cried, reaching out for him. "Please, Chad. I'll do whatever you want. Just let Christine go."

Andrea snickered as Chad grinned serenely. "Oh, I'm sure of that. Just do as I say. After all, you *are* my mate, right? Or did you forget that?"

She nodded. "I haven't forgotten that." She sobbed on that last word, inconsolable.

Chad touched her chin, bringing her gaze to look up into his eyes. "Good girl."

I felt like I was going to be sick.

He strode over to Emily, who had gone silent, the tears streaming down her cheeks. She didn't even acknowledge his presence. She just kept looking forward, begging me to do something. Anything.

I couldn't.

I heard the struggle behind me, of Colton trying to break free to stop what happened next, but I was immobilized, and the struggle ended as abruptly as it started.

No, no, no, no.

"You're the sacrifice, little one," Chad said, grinning down at Emily.

She spat in his face.

He grabbed her shoulder with a partially-transformed hand, and I watched in horror as his mouth changed to the trademark snout of a werewolf. He reared his head back and bit into the fleshy part of her neck.

Emily screamed.

My own muscles spurred, and I fought against my restraints, but the wolves held me fast. I could only watch. I heard a whimpering sound, and it took me a moment to realize that I was making the noise. I was crying.

Chad pulled back, wiping his bloodied mouth as it transformed back into a human's. Emily continued shrieking in pain as he walked away. She was turning white, and there was so much blood. It wasn't fatal, but it must have hurt a hell of a lot. If we didn't get her medical attention soon, it could very well turn into a big problem.

"Your turn, lover," Chad said to Sara.

My sister gulped, nodded, and walked over to Emily. She swayed on her feet as her friend looked up at her with pleading eyes. I wanted to scream at her to stop.

Sara hesitated, her eyes flicking over to me before she gave me a small, sad grin. I pleaded with her not to do it.

But then she bit into Emily's neck, the blood spurting between them. Emily's body went limp in the chair and Sara continued biting.

I can't believe this is happening. It can't!

Sara stepped back, heaving big breaths. She kept rubbing at her mouth, trying to wipe away the blood as if she herself couldn't believe what she had just done. She was shaking, almost as pale as Emily's unconscious form.

Then the wolves around me started howling.

Sara cast one last look back at me, before the transformation hit her. She threw her head back as fur sprouted and she fell to her knees. Her eyes went wide in fear as her entire body morphed, bones clicking into place, and her own muddied clothes ripped apart.

Standing before me, she was no longer Sara the Human, who was in control of all her functions and her humanity. I remembered that it took me a few times to really get a handle on my mountain lion instincts and control them.

She was Sara the Werewolf, a killing machine

And she turned her amber-colored gaze on me, and

licked her chops with a growl.

"Kill the werecat," Chad ordered smugly. "The one who's *different* here and trespassing on our pack's grounds."

Without another word, Sara pounced on me.

CHAPTER 16

I CHOSE THAT MOMENT TO PULL OUT MY last defense, even though it would make me far more vulnerable to injury. I called back my werecat, twisting out of the way as the wolves moved to give Sara access to me. By transforming, I granted myself a split second of reprieve as I slipped out of the other wolves' grasps.

The move worked, but just barely. I spun out of the way just as her teeth snapped in the air where I'd been only moments before.

"Sara," I pleaded, dodging another attack. "Remember who you are."

The wolf didn't answer, and instead lunged at me, her fangs bared. I ducked under it, transforming back into a werecat as I did so. Now, as we were both beasts, we were far more evenly matched, except for the fact that she was entirely wild and I still had my human faculties.

I hissed at her, hoping that would wake her up to the absurdity of this moment. She was a human in a wolf's body fighting a mountain lion for Pete's sake. Didn't that make her stop and think?

Apparently not.

She launched at me and I batted her out of the way. She was clumsy in this new body, and she kept slipping and tripping over her own paws. She shook her head with my last attack. I'd hit her hard and my heart broke for her.

I couldn't bear to hurt her again.

She barked and came at me again, a sign of an inexperienced werewolf. I used that to my advantage, sidestepping out of her way, and using my shoulder to flip her on her back. The movement both stunned and knocked the wind out of her, and I took that moment to pin her to the ground.

I screeched in her face, willing her with all of my might to put some sense into her damned head. She looked up at me, her eyes still wild.

I had one more option, one that I hated doing.

I transformed into a human, hoping that I had long enough to talk some sense into her while she was stunned.

And hopefully the other wolves wouldn't attack me as this happened.

"Sara, listen to me!" I yelled into her wolf-face. "Your name is Sara Driver, you're twenty-eight years old, and you're my sister. A human. Please, remember!"

She blinked up at me, the wild beast dissolving in front of me. I could watch as humanity crept its way back into her gaze as abject horror took over. She was herself. She remembered who she was and what she had done and what it meant from here on out.

I wanted to tell her that it was going to be all right, that we'd figure a way out of this. I still believed it. She had to as well.

I watched as her face and body morphed underneath mine. Tears filled her human eyes as she looked up. "Christine." Her voice broke. "I'm so sorry…"

And she passed out underneath me. I wanted to shriek in anger at the entire ordeal.

Except I didn't have much of a choice. A furry body slammed into me, and I sprawled across the floor, my own breath knocked out of me. I sobbed for breath as I laid on my back.

Being attacked by a shifter when you were human always sucked.

I turned my head to see Chad stalking over towards me, murder in his red eyes. This was it. This was going to be my end.

They say that your life flashes before your eyes before you die. I had too many regrets for that to happen—I didn't want to remember my mistakes, especially the ones that involved Shane. All I could think about was how I let Neptune down and how the new mermaids were going to be without a leader. Sara was going to have to live with this awful werewolf pack, and while I'd only known Colton for a day, we'd never get to explore if this attraction meant anything as far as relationships.

Because this bastard was going to kill me.

I steeled myself for it, even though I didn't want it to happen. I shut my eyes, ready.

It never came.

A roar sounded, this time unfamiliar as the scuffle and howls intensified again, and I snapped my eyes open. I turned my head to see Colton's werewolf form attack Chad's. Chad turned his murderous gaze on Colton, and they both growled and howled, circling each other. They were both of similar bulk and size. If they fought, one of them was going to die, and I couldn't risk it being Colton.

Not on my behalf. And not because of my sister's mistakes.

No. This was my fight. This was for me to end.

As I pushed myself up to a sitting position, I saw the throng of werewolves, including Andrea, move into position. *Attack* position. Apparently, after Sara and I fought, the ceasefire was over and they were moving into position to attack Colton. This time, they weren't going to restrain him or hold him hostage.

They'd just kill him.

I couldn't have that.

A surge of adrenaline brought me to my feet and I rushed at Chad, transforming back into a mountain lion as I did so. I caught Chad in the middle, grabbing him by the scruff of his neck. I hadn't expected to get this far, so this had caught both of us off-guard. He was too slow to respond, and the slightest twitch of my powerful jaws would collapse his windpipe and he'd be dead. I didn't even have to tear out his throat.

I had him at my mercy, and all I needed was to finish

him and be done with it. We both knew it, because I could see the whites of his eyes as he tried to look at me.

Except, in that moment, I realized that I couldn't do it. I was a mountain lion shifter due to a bad choice I made for love, but I wasn't a killer. Even though this bastard had terrorized my sister and her friends and who knew how many people, I couldn't bring myself to end it this way.

In that moment, I was more human than animal.

It drove me nuts, that I could end this now, but I couldn't do it. I hated it in movies when someone was stupidly benevolent, yet here I was.

I realized that I was still Christine, and I was not a killer.

I took my paw, and put it just underneath my jaw, and applied pressure to his throat, enough to make him gag. I released my jaws and called back my inner beast, shifting back into a human for the umpteenth time that night.

"Get out," I snarled at Chad. "I've won, and I'm letting you live. Get out of this warehouse. Get out of Atlanta. I don't want you around my sister anymore." I raised my voice so that everyone else in the warehouse could understand me. "And I want all of the other werewolves to lay off and leave us alone. Your leader is defeated. Now just walk away with dignity."

All of the other wolves watched me, their mouths agape. Chad snarled before nodding slowly.

I deliberated if he was telling the truth, but I couldn't very well hold him like this forever. I made a choice in that moment.

"Transform back into a human," I said, "and I'll let you go." His lip curled and I increased the pressure on his windpipe. "*Now.*"

I felt his body change underneath mine, but I didn't take my eyes off his face. If he was going to betray me, I would be able to read it in his face. When he was fully human again, I relaxed just a bit. It's amazing how less threatening someone can appear when they don't have huge teeth.

I pushed myself off him and got to my feet. I offered my hand to him, to let him know that I was in charge. This could go one of two ways, and I was prepared for either of them.

He chose the worse one.

He took my hand, but as I pulled him to his feet, he tried kicking my legs out from underneath me. I'd been expecting something like that. After I divorced Shane, I took jiu jitsu for self-defense because I needed it if he ever wanted to show his sorry face around me again.

When his leg connected with mine, I shifted my weight, spun him on his stomach, and smashed his face into the concrete ground.

"I told you to behave!" I yelled, holding him fast.

Apparently, there'd been enough force in that movement to knock him out cold. His entire body slumped underneath me as a rivulet of blood started spreading. Maybe I broke his nose. Maybe worse. I didn't care at that moment.

As I straightened up, I saw that the werewolves were all looking at me, shocked, like they'd never seen anyone defeat him before, much less a tall, skinny woman in her early thirties.

"You defeated our Alpha," the closest wolf said, shock in his voice.

"I had to," I said, not catching his drift. "He was trying to kill me."

"No, you don't understand," a wolf to my right replied. "You *defeated* our alpha. And you're a shifter. And that makes you…"

"*Our* Alpha?" another one asked, his voice raising in pitch. "Is that even possible?"

I searched the crowd, trying to find Colton's eyes to ask him for help. I jumped at the feathery touch of an uncertain hand on my arm. Colton was standing next to me in his human form as well. Except he was looking at me in the same way as the other werewolves. I wished he'd stop; I wish they'd all stop doing that.

"You defeated him, Christine," he whispered. "And not only that, you asserted your dominance over him."

Asserted my dominance? I just wanted to beat him into submission. Oh, wait, I'd said, "I told you to behave." Among other things. I now regretted my choice of words.

"And that makes me their Alpha?" I asked, panicked. "I'm not even a werewolf."

He combed a hand through his hair. "I don't know," he admitted softly. At least it was honest.

"Has that ever happened before?" another wolf asked.

"She's my leader," one of them said, kneeling in front of me. "It's how we do things."

I looked on in horror as all fifty wolves knelt in front of me.

And then I remembered I was naked in front of them. *Again.*

CHAPTER 17

COLTON RADIOED SOME BACK-UP TO COME to Old Plow Company to arrest Chad for domestic abuse, kidnapping, and assaulting an officer. All true allegations, although we bent the meanings slightly.

Andrea was also taken for accessory to kidnapping. I can't say that I didn't take a little bit of pleasure in that. She deserved whatever punishment was coming her way.

The cops drove both of them away in a cop car a short while ago. Chad glared daggers at me, but I knew from experience that it was all hot air.

He was going to jail, that was all that mattered.

Colton had also called an ambulance for Emily, who had woken up from Sara's bite. She was going to have to go into emergency surgery for the wound in her neck. In order to protect the identities of the werewolves and the shifter world in general, he had told the paramedics and the police that she'd been attacked by Chad's dog. Emily begrudgingly agreed with that story.

Nothing like lying to the authorities. Although, I guess Colton was a part of the law enforcement, so I'm not sure if it still counts.

Unfortunately, the paramedics asked if the dog that had bit her was rabid. I denied it, but since they didn't have a dog to test, I feared she'd be getting some shots in the near future for that.

At least she'd live. I don't think that she and Sara were going to be on speaking terms after this.

We sat out in the parking lot as the police cordoned off the crime scene. We had nowhere else to go, and I was glad for the respite, even though the flashing lights were giving me a headache. Now that everything was wearing off, I felt like I'd aged a hundred years. All I wanted was to curl up and fall asleep.

I was wearing another strange ensemble of clothing from Siouxsie, but it was my last change of clothes for the night, so they'd have to do. Sara leaned against a cop car, wearing Colton's spare shirt as a dress (there was no hope of the pants fitting, but the shirt reached her knees). She looked shell-shocked from the entire ordeal, and I didn't blame her.

After all, she was a werewolf now.

"Hey, you okay?" I asked her.

I watched as her jaw clenched and unclenched, but she said nothing. I sighed and combed a hand through my filthy hair.

I couldn't wait to get back to work. That would seem nice and relaxing compared to this. I wasn't sure what the kids would think of a mermaid that had a shiner and a bunch of cuts, but I knew a few tricks with makeup. I'd hidden bruises a long time ago, too.

"She was my neighbor…" Sara's voice trailed off as I looked at her, trying to follow her thoughts. "Andrea. She'd been my neighbor for the past five months, and we really hit it off. I can't help but think she was a plant. That Chad put her there to keep an eye on me."

I put my hand over hers and gave a quick squeeze. I'd been wondering that too, and I had come to the same conclusion. That Chad, in his megalomania, had become so obsessed with Sara, he had lined up his chess pieces to make a move a long time ago.

He just hadn't expected Sara to leave town during the full moon. Or her sister being a mountain lion shifter.

I still couldn't believe that Andrea was his sister. Or that Sara didn't see it.

"Even if she was," I said, "you're safe now." I made a mental note to be sure that Andrea was never going to bother her again.

Her eyes widened as she looked at me. "Am I?"

"Yes."

"You're the pack Alpha now."

I snorted in derision. Like hell I was.

I'd made one order as their pack alpha and that was for everyone who wasn't Chad to go home and get as far away from here as possible

My home was back in Jacksonville with the mermaids. I wasn't going to spend the rest of my life in Atlanta tied up with some wolves that I didn't even know. I'd had a lot of responsibility in my time, but I wasn't about to give up who I was because they were looking for someone else to lead them.

That, they'd have to do on their own.

"Hey. Are you okay?"

I looked up to see Colton looking down at me, concern in his eyes. Concern just for me. Sara slunk off, giving us our space. Even though she was most likely traumatized by what happened, she was still trying to play matchmaker.

My little sister had a one-track mind.

I crossed my arms and sighed. "Yeah. I'm just confused by everything that happened."

"You were...impressive back there," he said. "I can see why they want you to be their pack alpha."

"I'm not even a werewolf, Colton. I belong in Jacksonville."

"How can you say that?" he asked, looking down at me. "You're the leader of these wolves now."

"You take control of them. You're closer to Atlanta than I am. You're a werewolf!"

"You're not...?" His voice trailed off, and I saw the hurt in his eyes. "You're not even considering it?"

I shook my head. "They don't need a pack. They're adults. They can make their own decisions."

His mouth opened. "You're not even going to give it try? You're letting all of these people down."

"I'm not letting anyone down." I crossed my arms and looked away. "I don't want anything to do with them. I hereby give you authority to command them."

He swallowed, his throat clicking audibly. "It doesn't work that way, Christine."

"Tough."

He sighed. "Just…think on it."

I'd been living a different life because of the choices I made in the past. I wasn't about to change everything up again because these werewolves suddenly decided I was Mother Goose. I was only here to save my sister and friend. Nothing else.

"I'm not going to change my mind," I said, determined.

Colton's expression was hurt, but he turned away from me in a huff to talk to some other officers.

I guess that ruined any sort of thing that was developing between us. I shouldn't have gotten my hopes up. Not that it would have worked anyway with him in northern Georgia and me in Jacksonville. But I still felt a tightening in my chest at the thought of what might have been.

Sara was watching me silently. "Hey, Christine?"

I glanced at her. "Mmm?"

"Is Jacksonville really that great?"

CHAPTER 18

"I HONESTLY THOUGHT I'D NEVER SEE YOU back here," Neptune said, his weather-beaten face crinkling into a wide grin until I couldn't even see his eyes. "As I said, all of the other mermaids resigned after they left me."

I stepped into his office, shutting the door behind me. "Well," I said, "they hadn't been in it for ten years like me. This is my home." That I knew for certain now.

Neptune's expression fell. "You really are a good friend, Christine."

I felt my cheeks blush. "No, I'm not," I said guiltily.

I thought about all of the werewolves I left behind in Atlanta. We'd had a meeting at a bar the night after the debacle at Old Plow Company. Not only did I tell them that I couldn't be their pack leader, but I also told them that they didn't have to follow pack conventions. They didn't need an alpha to run their lives. They were in control of their own destinies now.

The concept seemed foreign to them. They didn't like the idea of striking out on their own and making their own paths in life. For most of their adult lives (and for some of them, most of their lives, period), they'd worked and lived as a unit, always deferring to their leader's choices. Chad had been the leader for only three years now, but he'd been just like the others before him.

They were resistant at first. They fought and begged me to stay. Colton was the biggest voice in trying to make me stay.

In the end, I had to do what was right for me. I had my own promises to keep at Neptune's World. I could never erase the memory of the looks of betrayal as I told them gently but firmly that I had my own life to live.

They were going to have to accept that.

"Yes, you are," Neptune said. "You wouldn't do anything you thought would harm others."

The werewolves certainly thought differently. "That's not true either."

He chuckled and got up from his chair. "Do you want a drink?" he asked, opening up the wet bar.

Neptune was an ex-sailor; a "drink" meant straight-up rum, like a pirate.

"I'm good, thanks."

He poured himself a glass of—I guessed correctly—rum. He took out another glass and poured a second. I guess I was going to get a glass too. I steeled myself for it.

"What happened to your eye, by the way?" he asked suddenly.

I blinked. I'd gotten so used to my swollen eye, I almost forgot about it. "Allergies," I said. "They got really bad up at the cabin."

That was code word for, "You don't want to know." And Neptune knew me well enough not to press the issue.

He cracked another smile at me before dissolving in a fit of coughing. I debated briefly on asking if I could help or grabbing a chair, but he waved me away before I could even act. "I'm fine," he said. "I'm fine."

"Did you get that looked at?" I said, remembering that the coughing was getting more and more prevalent.

"I have," he said gruffly.

"Oh." I shivered, hoping that there wasn't more to it.

"Do you want to know how your mermaids did while you were gone?" he asked, changing the subject again.

"I…hope they did all right?" I asked, feeling dread take hold of my stomach.

He blinked at me before laughing. He sat down at his desk, set my glass in front of me, and propped his feet up as he took a big swig of his rum. "They did wonderfully," he said. "They didn't miss a step, the crowd loved them, and they were flawless."

"That's wonderful," I said, relieved. I didn't pick up the rum.

"Seems like they don't need ol' Neptune around anymore," he said. "Which is a good thing."

His words caught me off guard. "What do you mean?" I asked, fearing what he was going to say before he said it.

He paused, every fiber of his being going stock-still for a moment before answering. "I'm dying, Christine." And he took another swig of his rum.

I blinked as the news hit me. "What?" I was numb. Nothing could penetrate the ice that covered my body. I didn't hear correctly—*surely I didn't hear correctly*.

Neptune coughed again. "That's what this cough is. I went to the doctor; I keep my promises." He gave me a pointed look. "Seems all those years of smoking have caught up with me." He coughed, more violently this time. It was enough to bring me to my feet.

He waved me down. "Gotta get used to that, Christine," he said. "I have four months left to live."

"They can't do anything about it?" I demanded. "When did this happen?"

"It's been off and on for several years now," he said. "I had lung cancer before you ever joined the mermaids. Had a lung removed. The whole nine yards. I beat it. At least, I *thought* I did. It's probably payback for the horrible things I've done in life." He took another drink. "It's back, and this time, there's nothing to do except get my affairs in order."

My eyes filled with tears. This couldn't be happening. He was my boss. He was one of my dearest friends. He couldn't die on me.

"Part of me getting my affairs in order," he said, "is deciding who will take over Neptune's World when I'm gone." He looked at me, his eyes sparkling. "I'm leaving it to you, Christine."

I didn't think I heard him right. "What?"

"Over the next few months, I'll introduce you to all

of the business side of things. Consider it a promotion for now, but when I'm gone, you'll be in charge of the aquarium." He chuckled mirthlessly. "Actually, you could change it to 'Christine's World', but you gotta admit, it doesn't have the same ring to it, does it?"

"I don't know if I can do that." My hands were shaking.

"Stop feeling like the world is ending around you," Neptune grumped. "You're a fine leader, Christine. Under your instruction, you've taught so many mermaids to perform. You know the ins and outs of this aquarium better than I do." He waggled his finger at me. "And you've been like a daughter to me over the past ten years."

"I can't...Neptune, I—"

He turned away from me, towards the window so he could look out the window. "It's already done. I talked to my lawyer while you were in Georgia. I figured if you came back, it meant that you were serious about this little world I created. I always knew I could count on you."

My bottom lip trembled.

"Cheer up, Christine," he said. "You'll be fine. I'll teach you everything you need to know. The company itself isn't in 100% perfect shape, but I think you'll bring a sensibility to it that I never did."

"I don't know if I can do that." I'd just shirked one responsibility for this. I didn't know if I could handle it. I was a professional mermaid, not an aquarium owner.

I thought about Mr. Stevens, the president of the Houston Aquarium who I met back in November. He'd been so consumed by money and greed that he had stopped looking at the aquarium as a place of fun and only looked at it as a money-making machine. Even to the point where he wrongfully sourced his dolphins.

Neptune only laughed. "You can. Now, let's toast to this new development, shall we?"

I picked up the glass, even though it felt wrong to toast something when my heart was breaking inside. Our glasses clinked, and I took a swig. The rum burned all the way down, which matched the way I felt about this whole thing.

And then I remembered the original reason why I came in here. "I have a question for you."

He raised an eyebrow. "Yes?"

"My sister Sara is looking for a job. She wanted to get out of Atlanta and have a change of scenery." *Not to mention get away from the Atlanta pack of wolves.* "I was wondering if she could get a job as a mermaid."

He laughed. "Well, what do you think?"

"I think she'd make a great fit." Sara had studied dance and was on the swim team when she was in high school, all the way through college. Her life choices had steered her away from that, but I truly felt that she could make a difference with the mermaids.

"Well," Neptune said, a big grin spreading across his face. "You're the boss, Boss."

EPILOGUE

FOUR WEEKS LATER

IT REQUIRED A LOT OF PRACTICE AND A LOT OF time getting Sara up to speed with the mermaid routines, but her first performance went flawlessly. I couldn't be prouder of her.

The five of us were in full costumes and we held onto the side of the aquarium in the arena, our routine finished. We had twirled, spun, and dove in perfect sync.

It was a great performance, not only to the audience, but to ourselves. Why hadn't we thought of having five mermaids before? Adding Sara to our roster just felt perfect.

Why did I ever doubt my team's ability to perform on par with the old mermaids?

Because you're a control freak, Christine.

I might have to change that permanently. As I waved at the audience, I made that promise. I was going to live every day to the fullest.

The lights blinded us to the audience, but I saw the cameras flashing beyond it. I could also see Sara's face. It held pure joy. There was no other word for it. For the first time in a long time, she was at peace. Her eyes glittered with excitement as she faced the cheering crowd.

It also helped that she was away from the toxicity of the pack and her old life up in Atlanta. Not that the pack was bad, but she had been so traumatized by the events, I didn't think she'd ever set foot inside of Atlanta city limits ever again.

For now, she was staying in my tiny one-bedroom apartment in downtown Jacksonville, which was completely fine. She was welcome to stay as long as she needed in order to get her feet underneath her. That first full moon after her transformation into a werewolf was hard. We'd both transformed and went running out in a state park. But she told me that she wasn't going to let it define her. She was Sara Driver, professional mermaid now. Admittedly, being a professional mermaid didn't pay as well as her job at the PR firm, but that didn't matter anymore.

She was home. And I think after a while, I could segue her into a PR role as well so that we could get the word out about our work and ocean conservation. In that case, the performing-mermaid part was an added bonus.

Emily had called her once since our camping trip. She had moved to Austin to get away from everything. I didn't have the heart to tell her that there were shifters in Austin too. It was a pity, because I really liked her. I hoped she found what she was looking for.

I winked at Sara as we all slid back underneath the

waves, muffling the sounds of the audience. We swam underneath the surface, only surfacing when we were on the other side of the curtain that cordoned off the stage side of the tank to the backstage part.

Neptune was waiting for us, a huge grin on his face. He was clapping, his applause drowned out with the audience's. But I knew that he was extremely pleased.

"Wonderful job," he exclaimed, helping Murphy out of the water. He coughed and covered it up with his hand. Now that I knew the reason for the coughing, each one felt like a pang to my heart, like each one was a grain of sand in his time left with us. The both of us had decided not to tell the others about his illness. Why would we? All they'd do is fret and worry, wasting the precious last few months of his life

I knew that would happen because that was exactly what I was doing. I tried not letting it get to me, but I felt like I was losing a father and the one person who had helped me through the worst times of my life.

"How'd I do, Boss?" Sara asked as I helped her out of the water. She was still having trouble getting in and out of her silicon tail, so we always ended up dragging her onto dry land and helping her out.

"Perfect," I said. "You did wonderful."

She beamed at me. Yep, this was going to be a great transition for her. Not to mention, when we went on tour again in October, she'd get to see parts of North America that she'd never been to before.

I couldn't wait.

"Ms. Driver," an usher named Rachel said, putting her hand lightly on my arm. Ever since the news that I'd been promoted to Senior VP of something-or-other, everyone I had once been acquaintances with now called me that. It made me cringe, but I didn't correct her. "There's someone here to see you."

I shimmied out of my tail, careful not to tear the silicon. "Who is it?" I asked.

Rachel shrugged. "He wouldn't say."

I grinned at Sara. "Probably another local reporter on recruiting a fifth mermaid." The local papers always latched onto any news story about us mermaids—it was great for family articles. "I'll be right back. If he's hot, do you want me to get his number for you?"

"Maybe for yourself," Sara shot back as I got to my feet. I tied a floor-length sarong around my waist—it wouldn't do for a kid to see me without my tail. Things like that ruin the illusion.

I headed out from the backstage area towards the dressing room.

And paused as soon as I saw him in the hallway.

"Colton," I breathed.

"Hey," he said softly. He shifted a bouquet of flowers in his arms as he closed the distance between us.

He looked... *good*. Dapper, even, in a plaid shirt and a pair of tight jeans that his legs filled out oh-so nicely. I forced myself to focus on his face, which was shaded by the brim of his hat. Part of his right ear was missing, but that gave him a roguish look. I liked it.

I was suddenly conscious that I had shown up in my bikini and sarong, but I guess he'd seen more than that last month.

Still I crossed my arms. "Good to see you," I said honestly, even as my heart skipped a beat. "Did you see the show just now?"

"I did. That was…quite the performance," he said, giving me a wolfish smile. "Who knew that cats liked the water so much?"

I laughed as the awkwardness melted away. "Big cats like water. And apparently wolves," I added. "Did you see that Sara's now a professional mermaid?"

"I did. She did great. You did…awesome."

I chuckled at his word choice. I'd also been a mermaid for ten years, so of course I had the routine down pat. But he didn't need to know that. I would let him think that I was "awesome".

I nodded at the flowers. "Are those for me?"

His eyes sparkled for a moment before my question sunk in and jumped as if noticing them for the first time. "Uh, yeah. These are for you."

He handed the bouquet to me and I graciously took them, inhaling deeply. "You know these are tiger lilies, right?"

"Yeah." He stuffed his hands in his pockets, which, for a big man, made him seem like he was being sheepish.

"I looked around for mountain lion lilies, but those don't exist."

"They're beautiful."

"*You're* beautiful."

"I never pegged you for a romantic."

He shrugged. "I figured I should at least try. Because of how we left things."

That sobered my mood, and I sighed. "Listen, Colton…"

"I never should have expected you to stay," he blurted out. "That was rude of me."

"I should have handled it differently, though." I sighed. "I should have stayed and made sure they could stand on their own. They need a leader. It's my responsibility. I just…"

He put his broad hands on my shoulder and beckoned me to look up at him. "You're needed as a leader here, too. Besides, they're doing well. I think they're having trouble adapting to a life without an alpha, but they're doing all right. I've been working with them. I think they're picking up a mountain lion shifter's way of life."

That was true. I'd been in contact with them a few times over the last month. I told them that they could call me at any time and I'd help out. Even though I wasn't their leader, they still turned to me for advice. I guess I was going to have to get used to leadership, what with Neptune's death imminent.

I brushed that thought from my mind. "And you?"

His face fell. "I'm not doing so well," he admitted. "Been doing a lot of soul searching. I quit my job as a park ranger."

I blinked at him. "What?"

"I realized that I'd been stuck in the same groove for too long. That, as a pack alpha, I wasn't giving myself the chance to live fully. Stephen's death had impacted me a lot, but he wouldn't want me to feel trapped."

I raised an eyebrow. "You feel trapped? Out in a state park?"

He shrugged. "There are different kinds of cages than ones with bars."

Very true. I licked my lips. "Are you sure about that?"

"It's been done." He stuffed his hands into his pockets. "I turned in my two weeks' notice last Monday. I took a job at the Okefenokee National Wildlife Refuge."

I frowned. "Where's that?"

"About forty-five minutes northwest of here. Across the Georgia state line."

I let out a breath, trying to erase the skipping of my heart. Because it was racing so very fast. "It'd be two hours with Jacksonville traffic."

He leaned into me. "Still. It puts me that much closer to you."

"Why?"

He grunted in irritation and combed his hair. "Are you going to make me come out and say it?"

I gave him an innocent look. "Say what?"

He sighed. "I…like you. And don't go thinking that I up and quit my job to move here because of you. It was for me and finding myself, I promise." That wolfish grin was back. "The chance to ask you on a date was an added benefit."

"And what does Siouxsie think of this?"

He laughed. "Oh, she was livid that I abandoned the pack and put her back in charge of it."

"She's the alpha now?"

"Yep. And she ain't happy about it. She wants you to call her so she can chew you out for corrupting her grandson."

"I'd like that."

Truthfully, I would. His grandmother helped save my life, and I liked my brief time with her. And, standing here, I realized that I could most likely see her again, if whatever this was between us blossomed.

"So about that chance for a date…" I said carefully.

"I thought you'd never ask."

"Me ask?" I laughed. "I thought you were a gentleman."

"I had the impression that it didn't matter who asked who out. Besides, I'm new in town, I wouldn't have the foggiest idea of where to take you out."

He had a point there. "All right, then. Colton Donnelly, would you like to go to Olive Garden with me?"

He made a face as I hooked my arm through his. "I was hoping someplace more romantic."

"There's nothing more romantic than unlimited salad and breadsticks."

He laughed. "On one condition, and I consider this research for knowing what I'm getting into." I raised an eyebrow. "You tell me what happened between you and Mr. Were Mountain Lion."

He meant Shane. I'm grateful to say that the memory of my past didn't hurt so much anymore. I guess the events out in the Georgia wilderness made me stop regretting things. And even though it was an incredibly prying question, especially from a man I didn't know very well, I told him.

"He physically and emotionally beat me for the two years that I was a mountain lion with him," I said flatly. "I challenged him to a fight in front of his friends. As werecats. He didn't think I would win, but I showed him up. Told him if I saw his crummy face again, I'd do worse. Humiliated him in front of his friends and I haven't seen him since, except for the divorce proceedings."

It felt like a weight was off my chest.

He looked down at me, impressed. "I thought you were pretty spectacular out there. You're a fighter."

"Oh yeah," I warned. "I'm not afraid of mountain lions, and you can be damned sure that I'm not afraid of wolves."

He looked down at me, his blue eyes sparkling. "I'll keep that in mind."

The adventure concludes in…

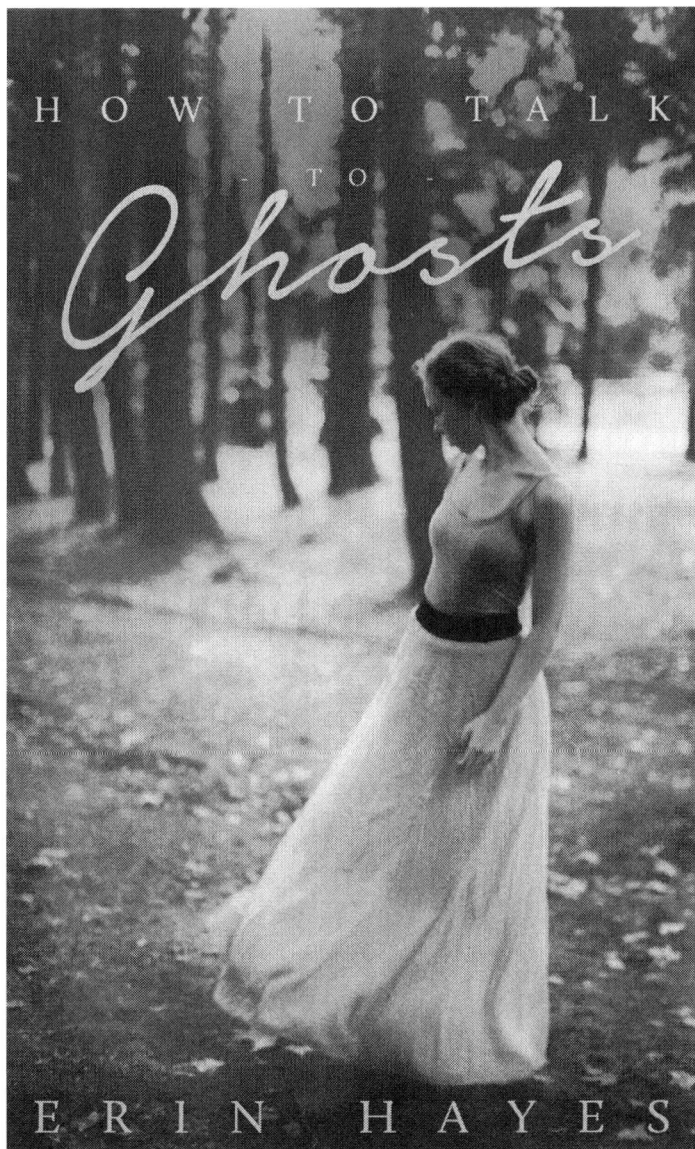

HOW TO TALK
- TO -
Ghosts

ERIN HAYES

Coming Soon.

ABOUT THE AUTHOR

Sci-fi junkie, video game nerd, and wannabe manga artist Erin Hayes writes a lot of things. Sometimes she writes books.

She works as an advertising copywriter by day, and she's a New York Times and USA Today Bestselling Author by night. She has lived in New Zealand, Hawaii, Texas, Alabama, and now San Francisco with her husband, cat, and a growing collection of geek paraphernalia.

You can reach her at erinhayesbooks@gmail.com and she'll be happy to chat. Especially if you want to debate Star Wars.

Follow her on:
www.erinhayesbooks.com
www.facebook.com/erinhayesbooks
Join her street team at: http://www.facebook.com/
groups/erinsnerdcrew/

Made in the USA
Lexington, KY
01 February 2017